THE NEW ENEMY

www.**totallyrandombooks**.co.uk

Titles by Andy McNab:

The New Recruit
The New Patrol

DROPZONE
Dropzone
Dropzone: Terminal Velocity

BOY SOLDIER (with Robert Rigby)
Boy Soldier
Payback
Avenger
Meltdown

For adults:
Bravo Two Zero
Immediate Action
Seven Troop
Spoken from the Front
The Good Psychopath's Guide to Success (with Professor Kevin Dutton)
Today Everything Changes

Novels:
Aggressor
Battle Lines (with Kym Jordan)
Brute Force
Crisis Four
Crossfire
Dark Winter
Dead Centre
Deep Black
Exit Wound
Firewall
Fortress
Last Light
Liberation Day
Recoil
Red Notice
Remote Control
Silencer
War Torn (with Kym Jordan)
Zero Hour

ANDY McNAB

THE NEW ENEMY

DOUBLEDAY

THE NEW ENEMY
A DOUBLEDAY BOOK
Hardback: 978 0 857 53342 5
Trade Paperback: 978 0 857 53343 2

Published in Great Britain by Doubleday,
an imprint of Random House Children's Publishers UK
A Penguin Random House Company

This edition published 2015

1 3 5 7 9 10 8 6 4 2

Copyright © Andy McNab, 2014
Front cover artwork and design © Stephen Mulcahey, 2014
Cover photography © Jonathan Ring, 2014

With thanks to David Gatward

The right of Andy McNab to be identified as the author of this work has been asserted
in accordance with the Copyright, Designs and Patents Act 1988.

Penguin Random House is committed to a sustainable future for our business,
our readers and our planet. This book is made from Forest Stewardship Council® certified paper.

Set in 13/17.5pt Adobe Garamond by Falcon Oast Graphic Art Ltd

RANDOM HOUSE CHILDREN'S PUBLISHERS UK
61–63 Uxbridge Road, London W5 5SA

www.randomhousechildrens.co.uk
www.totallyrandombooks.co.uk
www.randomhouse.co.uk

Addresses for companies within The Random House Group Limited can be found at:
www.randomhouse.co.uk/offices.htm

THE RANDOM HOUSE GROUP Limited Reg. No. 954009

A CIP catalogue record for this book is available from the British Library.

Printed and bound in Great Britain by Clays Ltd, St Ives plc

To all the Liams out there, and to the Ministry of Defence for their help and guidance to ensure this book reflects the true life of a young soldier

Glossary

AK47 – assault rifle, first developed in the USSR by Mikhail Kalashnikov

ACOG – Advanced Combat Optical Gunsight, providing up to 6x fixed power magnification, illuminated at night by an internal phosphor

Al Shabaab – terrorist group, affiliated with Al Qaeda. Based in Somalia, the group is fighting an insurgency against the recognized Somali federal government

Apaches – attack helicopters; gunships

battalion – a military unit, normally comprising between 650 and 750 infantry soldiers

BATUK – British Army Training Unit in Kenya

bayonet – a knife designed to fit in, on, over or underneath the muzzle of a rifle

bergen – name given to a large rucksack used by soldiers to carry sufficient equipment to allow them to survive for a number of days in theatre

blue on blue – a term for friendly fire, where weapon systems are inadvertently used on friendly forces rather than the enemy

camel bak – a large water reservoir that can be carried in a soldier's backpack

Camp Bastion – a fortified base for the Coalition Forces in the Helmand Province of Afghanistan

CFT– the Combat Fitness Test

CTR – Close Target Recce

CQR – Close Quarter Recce

Chinook – a helicopter which is most often used for transporting equipment or troops; known by soldiers as 'cows'

contact – any action involving the enemy and the discharge of weapons

dead-letter drop – a secret location used to pass items between individuals/groups while maintaining operational security

FOB – Forward Operating Base

Glock 17 Gen 4 – a lightweight and accurate pistol with a magazine capacity of 17 9mm rounds

ground sight – a term used for keeping a keen eye on the ground ahead for anything unusual

HESCO – multi-cellular wall units, filled with whatever material is available to hand, such as sand, and used to protect patrol bases. Tested against charges of up to 20,000lb

IED – an Improvised Explosive Device, which can be placed on the ground or used by suicide bombers;

GLOSSARY

sometimes activated by remote control

INT – army term for intelligence; information collected on, for example, enemy movements

KDF – the Kenyan Defence Force

khat – plant with amphetamine-like stimulant properties, which can be chewed

KIA – Killed In Action

LRCC – British Army's Light Reconnaissance Commander's Course

Lynx Mk7 – a multi-purpose military helicopter

MOD – Ministry of Defence

MP5 – 9mm submachine gun built by Heckler & Koch

NCO – Non-Commissioned Officer, like a corporal or sergeant

PRR – Personal Role Radio: small transmitter-receiver radio that enables soldiers to communicate over short distances, and through buildings and walls

Recce Platoon – comprising soldiers who have completed the LRCC and who work ahead of front-line combat units, looking for enemy units and reporting their positions to their commanders

reconnaissance – the process of obtaining information and intelligence (INT) about an enemy

RPG – Rocket-Propelled Grenade

SA80 – the standard British Army assault rifle, made by Heckler & Koch

GLOSSARY

SAS – Special Air Service, tasked to operate in difficult and often changing circumstances, sometimes in absence of guidance and within situations that have significant operational and strategic importance

SCAR – Special Operations Forces Combat Assault Rifle, a modular rifle available in both 5.56mm and 7.62 calibres

Sharpshooter – a highly accurate rifle, taking a 7.62 round, able to hit a target at up to 800 metres

SLR – a top-spec camera with a powerful zoom lens

stress position – an interrogation technique whereby the human body is forced into a position that places most of its weight on only a small number of muscles. For example, squatting with thighs parallel to the ground

subsurface surveillance op – carrying out surveillance from a position dug into the ground and camouflaged

theatre – field of operations within a war

tour – period of active service; a normal tour in Afghanistan would be approximately six months

UKSF – UK Special Forces. Term used to encompass the wide range of special forces units across the Army, Royal Navy and Royal Air Force

1

Present Day 1 a.m.
Somewhere on the Welsh Borders

The night sky was a grumbling black mass of boiling clouds, rain pouring onto an already sodden earth. Liam Scott had been on the run for most of the night now and he was starting to lose track of time. But all he was really concerned about was staying one step ahead of those who were out to catch him. Because when they did, the real pain would start.

Dressed in a heavy, ankle-length trench coat, ill-fitting clothes, and boots that rubbed his feet and were tied to his ankles by bailer twine, he was completing the escape and evasion training part of the LRCC. Before joining the course he hadn't given much thought to what it would involve and in some ways he was glad of that. If he'd known then what he knew now, he'd have had more than a few sleepless nights thinking about it.

It was meant to be tough. In fact, not just tough, but utter hell. OK, so he knew he wasn't about to get water-boarded or have his teeth smashed in, but that was no consolation. He knew he would get caught. He also knew once that happened a team of interrogators were going to put him through the mill. There was no mess-ing with any of the training he'd gone through, but this was designed specifically to try and break you, mentally, physically and psychologically. If you couldn't hack it, then you didn't get through, simple as that. You were binned, sent back to your battalion.

Pausing for a breather, Liam hid under the low branches of a fir tree, a tattered and torn thing that looked about as happy with the weather as he felt him-self. He ran through the theory and practical training they had all received before being sent out on the exercise proper. It had been a lot of fun in many ways, and pretty interesting too: all about eating wild food, using the stars and the landscape for navigation, real *Boy's Own* stuff, like they were all on a Scout Camp. Now, though, having been rounded up and thrown out of the back of a truck one at a time on an undisclosed route, with a shitty hand-drawn map, all that stuff seemed not just a long time ago, but to Liam at that moment, next to useless. He couldn't read the stars because there weren't any, thanks to the cloud and rain, the landscape bore little resemblance to the map he was trying to use, and stopping to find some lovely wild nuts and berries to nibble on just wasn't an option. He was running for his life.

Shouts from his left had Liam moving on again and running hard. His feet hurt like hell, he was cold, and the coat, tied round his waist with frayed rope, was heavy and cumbersome. His dark hair, cut military short, was slick with sweat and he knew it was only a matter of time before he was caught, but that was no reason to give up. He had to make the chase good, work like a fox ahead of the hounds, do his damnedest to keep running as long as he could.

He kept to the cover of the trees, did his best to make as little sound as possible, but it was difficult with branches clawing at him, cutting him, scratching his face with every step. The dark and the rain didn't help either. He had no torch, and the land around him was all shadows. He lost count of the number of times he tripped up, smashed his head into a branch.

Ahead, Liam saw a change in the darkness indicating the trees were coming to an end. From then on it was open ground, for a while at least. He dropped low, paused, sucked oxygen into his lungs. He couldn't go right – the voices were still closing in. And he couldn't turn back. It was left or straight on, and both options were, to his mind, piss poor. He wondered how many of the other lads had already been caught – if he'd be the first.

Crunching his eyes tight shut, he psyched himself to make a break from the trees. The next cover he could make out would be a stone wall. If he reached it, he would then follow it left to a small rise, keeping low all the way, then down into a shallow ditch, which would no doubt be knee deep in freezing cold mud.

With a final deep breath he sprang forward like a jackrabbit, bolting away from the tree line and going hell for leather towards the wall. Blood pounded in his ears, his feet barely managing to keep him upright across the rough ground. He didn't look back, just kept his eyes on the wall, and it was getting closer. He could make this. Had to.

The ground beneath Liam's left foot disappeared and he stumbled. Rabbit hole or just a dip in the soft ground, he didn't know, but it had screwed his escape. He tumbled forwards and landed hard, slamming his face into mud, grit, stone. Air spewed out of him, his lungs emptying as pain and fear crackled through him like electricity. But it wasn't over yet and Liam was back up on his feet and moving.

The wall was close now and he kept on, forcing his

legs to move faster, gulping air, wiping rain and muck and probably blood from his face.

The wall came up quicker than he expected, but any sense of achievement was shot to pieces as, from behind it, grey shadows swooped in for him like crows. Hands grabbed him and he was dropped to the ground, someone on his back, snapping his wrists together with a plastic quick tie, another pulling a hessian sack over his head.

Shit . . .

Voices came at him – loud and hard and violent – but Liam wasn't listening, knew there was no point. Dragged and pushed and punched forwards, he was then heaved into the back of a truck.

He knew what was coming. And he wasn't looking forward to it.

The sack over Liam's head stank of sweat and mould and fetid water. After a hellish journey, he'd been dragged out onto the ground like a sack of coal. Then, next to blind, thanks to the sack, he'd been pushed, half tripping, half running, into what he guessed from the echoes of his footsteps on the ground was a room of some kind. And all the way harsh voices had yelled at him, screaming insults, swearing, threatening violence.

'Name?'

The voice was a Rottweiler's snarl. Liam didn't recognize it at all and that put him even more on edge. This was a training exercise and he'd expected it to be carried out by the staff from the LRCC. So who the holy hell was this?

'I said name, you deaf fuck!'

A hand caught Liam across the back of the head. It wasn't hard, but it was enough to make him flinch and he immediately cowered.

'Christ, you are fucking deaf, aren't you? *NAME!*'

Liam gave the information asked for, but nothing else. As they'd all been told in training, under the Geneva Convention, there was a strict protocol on the information they were actually required to give.

'So where are you from, Scott?'

Liam repeated his name, but another slap caught him.

'Actually, fuck that bollocks,' said the voice. 'We already know where you're from, and all about your mummy and daddy. Got all that information already from one of the other lads. Spewed it out like a fucking pussy. He's binned. You will be too.'

Liam was trying to zone out. He knew they were simply doing their best to wind him up, get him to react. He had to remain strong. It was a mind game.

'Daddy's a bit of a bastard, it seems,' the voice

continued. 'Didn't think his lad would make the army. Well, looks like he's right, doesn't it? You're a failure, Scott, aren't you? Nineteen years old, and already a total fucking failure. How you got this far I haven't a clue, you useless piece of shit.'

'Scott, Liam, Lance Corp—'

It wasn't a slap this time that cut him short, but a soft kick to the back of his knees. It buckled him and sent him hard to the floor. His knees took the impact and pain stabbed up through his body.

'First you fuck up with that ration bag, then you screw your CFT. You're binned, mate, you hear me? So just give up now and save us all a lot of time. You'll be doing yourself a favour.'

Binned? thought Liam. What the fuck was this goon on about? They couldn't bin him. He hadn't failed, he couldn't have done.

'Get this wanker out of my sight!' the voice said. 'Fucksake – why does the army waste my time with tossers like this?'

Hands grabbed Liam and he was dragged away from the room and the voice which was now laughing. Then he was pulled up and forced to stand in a semi-crouched position, arms held straight above his head. Icy water was thrown on him – the shock of it knocked the breath from his chest. Then what silence there was in that moment was broken by a blast of white noise. It was deafening and disorientating, and he couldn't block it out. Soon his head started to throb with pain.

Liam's arms ached and his legs wanted to give way, but every time he moved in the slightest bit, hands would put him back into the same position and more water would be thrown over him.

He had no idea how many people were around him, if he was going to get slapped again, or from what direction. Then, after what seemed like an eternity, he was dragged once more into the room with the voice.

Liam heard paper being shuffled.

'Says here your mate Cameron got blown to pieces on your first tour,' said the voice. 'What kind of soldier lets that happen, Scott? Where the fuck were you when he got hammered by an RPG?'

Liam did his best to zone out, but the mention of the death of his friend had caught him off guard. Memories came at him like bullets, smashing into him, forcing him to remember.

'I'll tell you where you were,' said the voice. 'Looking after yourself, that's where. All you give a shit about is yourself. And if there's a chance of a medal, all the better, right?'

Liam wanted to yell back that it hadn't been like that. He'd been there with Cam, held his smashed body as they'd waited for him to be medevac'd out. He could still smell the blood, the smoke, the burned flesh.

'Cat got your tongue?'

Liam breathed out then said his name, rank, number.

'Oh, just fuck off,' said the voice.

Once again, rough hands grabbed Liam and he was dragged out and forced into another stress position.

And so it continued, interrogations followed by stress positions, the insults and wind-ups growing ever worse and more personal. He was stripped naked and laughed at, told the rest of the lads had already quit and were waiting on him to do the same so they could get home and warm. Then, with no warning at all, there was a change of tack.

Liam's hood was yanked off.

'This is where it gets interesting,' said the man sitting behind the desk in front of him. He was wearing plain army fatigues, but there was no insignia to give away regiment or rank. Steely-eyed, whoever he was, Liam wasn't convinced by the snake-like smile that sat on the man's face. 'What will it take to get you to talk, eh?'

Liam heard scuffling behind him as another man was brought in, hooded just like he had been. He too was silent, remembering his training, thought Liam, though that made it utterly impossible for him to tell who it was.

The man behind the desk stood up and removed his pistol from his leg holster.

'You going to talk?' he asked.

Liam was staring at the weapon. What the fuck was going on?

The man nodded and the two soldiers who had brought the hooded figure in forced him to his knees.

'Tell me, Scott,' said the interrogator. 'Is the loss of another man's life something you can live with?'

Liam squeezed his eyes shut, shook his head. This was going too far now, surely. What were they playing at? His mind was muddled and his grasp on reality was slipping.

'I asked you a question, Scott,' said the man, and pointed the weapon at the head of the man on his knees.

'No!' said Liam suddenly, the word out before he could do anything to stop it.

'Oh, so you can speak!'

'You're taking the piss!' said Liam. 'This is just a fucking exercise!'

'Oh, is it?' asked the man. 'You sure about that? You sure that any of us in here are legit? What if we're not, you thought of that? What if we're dangerous fuckers who've nabbed you and have been playing you a line all along? I mean, it wouldn't be difficult, would it? A bit of observation and we'd know where to find you, where to hit hard, and where to take you. And here you are, all alone.'

Liam was trying to think, to sort truth from fiction, but he was so tired and disorientated that he started to wonder if what he was hearing was right. What if the exercise had been blown? What if all this was for real and he was in the hands of some home-grown terrorists just looking for any intelligence they could get their hands on about how the army operated?

The man readied his weapon. 'I'm serious, Scott,' he said.

'You can't!' Liam yelled. 'You fucking can't!'

The man on his knees started to cry, his whimpering, stuttering howls setting Liam's teeth on edge.

'Who the fuck are you to tell me what I can and can't do, eh?' shouted the interrogator. 'Who? Tell me! Tell me everything about yourself, your family, your training, you hear? Everything!'

'I can't!' Liam yelled back. 'I just can't!'

Then he was dragged back out of the room, hood over his head, and a minute later back in a stress position. It was all he could do not to collapse and give up.

'Hungry, Liam?'

He could smell it – bacon and coffee.

Once again he was back in that room, hood off, and

staring at the man who had held a pistol at another person's head the last time.

'You've done well, Liam,' the man said. 'Thought we had you for a moment there. Have a seat and a bite to eat. The coffee is warm and sweet. Just what you need, right?'

Liam hesitated. What was going on? He could hardly think straight now. His body was in agony and his mind slowly fraying.

'Come on, mate.' The man smiled. 'What harm can it do? Sit down. Relax. It'll do you good. Then we can talk, right? Like human beings?'

The bacon butty looked delicious and the coffee was sending Liam's senses crazy. Was the exercise over? Still he didn't move.

'You must be starving. Take it.'

Liam's brain was addled by what he'd gone through, but it was still sparking. What if something was in the food, the drink? It could be drugged. Even if it wasn't, surely they were just trying to break him a bit more, right? Have him relax, drop his defences just a little?

'This is your last chance, mate,' said the man. 'Come on now, do us all a favour and stop this nonsense. We can have you back in a warm bed before you know it. You don't really want this, do you? And how much more do you think you can handle?'

'Scott, Liam,' said Liam, holding onto what sanity he had left. 'Lance Corporal—'

'I know what fucking rank you are, you twat!' the man yelled, and he grabbed the sandwich and threw it across the room. 'You think this is a fucking game? Our job is to break you, you cocky little bastard! Now get the fuck out of my sight!'

Dragged from the room, hood pulled over his head once again, Liam was forced to stand, half bent forwards, arms stretched out in front of him. The pain was now unbearable, but still he was kept from falling to the ground. He found himself drifting off into memories he felt safe in. They were all of his time in the army, the happiest time of his life so far.

Hanging out in an FOB in Afghanistan, chatting with the lads about what they'd done that day, taking the piss out of each other, wondering about the day ahead.

Talking to his mates.

But that was in the battalion, back in 4 Rifles. He never should have left. Since he'd got it into his head that he might make selection for Recce Platoon and started this fucking Light Reconnaissance Commander's Course, things had just gone to shit . . .

2

Two weeks earlier

'Scott, mate, you're on.'

Liam opened his eyes, switching from comatose to fully alert in a beat. The air was cold and his face icy. It was raining. He was lying in his doss bag in a well-camouflaged hole big enough to hide himself, three other soldiers, and enough kit to keep them alive for upwards of a week or more. It was Liam's first time carrying out an operation from a subsurface observation post, or OP. And so far, apart from the rain, it was going well. If this went to plan he'd be moving up soon to CTR and getting in close to the enemy.

Two of the soldiers were still out cold, though they weren't exactly being covert about it. The other, Corporal Finn Cordner, who had the build of a greyhound, had spent the past two hours staring through a spotting scope and snapping photographs with an SLR. It was now Liam's turn.

'What a bloody racket,' whispered Liam, careful to keep his voice low and quiet as he heaved himself out of his bag to take over Cordner's position. 'How are we supposed to avoid detection if they keep on snoring like that? They'll be heard for miles!'

Cordner shrugged. 'I've had to keep kicking the dozy bastards to keep it down,' he said, the words spoken in a soft Irish accent. 'Reckon you should be tested for snoring before you do this kind of job. Imagine getting slotted because your mates snore! How shite would that be?'

'And they've been like that all night?'

'It's like being in a hole with a fucking whoopee cushion and a properly excited pig trying to hump it to death,' said Cordner. 'And the stink coming out of Biggsy's arse has got to be banned as a chemical weapon under the Geneva Convention. And if it isn't, it bloody well should be. The filthy bastard.'

'What about the target? Seen anything?' Liam asked, as Cordner got himself as close to comfortable as was possible.

'Minimal,' Cordner replied. 'Just a few sentries and no regular patrols. I've recorded the timings, but there seems to be no set routine yet. They're obviously keeping it random. But in this past hour activity has increased. Something's up, so keep eyes on whatever it is they're doing. Could be big. Then again, it could all amount to nothing and we'll have spent our time freezing our balls off and collecting our own shit for nothing.'

Liam carefully moved himself up to the edge of the hole and stared down the long-range spotting scope, the kind used by snipers; beside him was a top-spec SLR camera with a seriously capable zoom lens. The OP was situated up on a small tree-covered rise. Below them, and about 800 metres away, was a collection of buildings. It was their job to sit tight, remain undiscovered, and gather as much intelligence – or INT as they called it – as they could about what it was and who was using it. And that meant twenty-four-hour observation, which included sketching out maps, photographing and recording absolutely every detail they could, before pulling out and heading back to base.

Dawn was smearing the blackness of the night into a dull ocean grey and Liam was now able to get a better view of what they were there to observe. Above him, the roof of their hide was covered in netting threaded with vegetation. Odds were if anyone walked by, the only way they'd find it would be by falling in.

'Burger and beans,' said Cordner, quickly tucking into his army rations before grabbing some shuteye. 'My favourite. Want some?'

Liam quickly followed Cordner's lead. He was starving, and even though heating the food was out of the question – you don't go digging a hole to hide in, then announce your location with smoke and steam and the smell of food – he still pushed it into his face with relish.

Cordner's hand appeared in front of Liam. It was holding a small red bottle like it was about to explode.

Liam took the bottle. The label read 'Tabasco'.

'Gives it a bit more of a kick,' said Cordner. 'Never leave home without it. I reckon I've become even more addicted to it since giving up smoking a few months ago. But too much Tabasco will give you a serious case of the shits. And that's not good when you're on this kind of OP, is it?'

Liam smiled. He had already learned that everything you took into the OP with you, you took back out. No trace was to be left behind. And that meant, at its most basic, primitive level, crapping into a bag, dropping it into your bergen, and hoping to God it didn't burst on the way back out. Everyone knew the horror stories of badly tied bags, bags getting holes in, soldiers with the shits.

Food finished, Cordner got into his sleeping bag.

'Sweet dreams,' said Liam, his own food now finished, not turning to watch Cordner drift off. He picked up the long-range spotting scope again.

The rain continued, freefalling out of the dark, the roof doing little to protect any of them from the elements. Liam brought his hands up to his mouth, blowing warm air across them in an attempt to bring them back to life. They were numb, both with the cold and the wet, and from the hours digging the hole, and he could feel nothing. Not even a phosphorous grenade burning for almost a minute at a blistering 5000 degrees Fahrenheit would warm them up, he thought.

For the next couple of hours, Liam silently observed the target below them. It was a collection of old farm buildings, all overgrown, with sections of roof that had given way to time and the weather. Where farm animals had once lived, soldiers now moved about. They'd been out there on the OP for four days now, thought Liam. Something had to happen soon.

Armed men in combat gear were patrolling a perimeter. And Cordner had been right, Liam observed. There was no set timing to the patrols, as though they were doing their best to ensure that anyone observing them would never be able to find a clear time when the place could be attacked. That in itself made him uneasy.

He took regular snapshots with the SLR, slowly filling up its memory card. They had a stack of others with them, so he didn't need to worry about saving memory space. He also mapped the area on a pad of waterproof paper, marking down the location of the buildings, other objects, both natural and man-made, the distances measured through the gradients on the lens of the spotting scope, the positions and movements of the soldiers.

At least, that's what he was supposed to be doing, but Liam was finding it hard to see any correlation between what he was drawing and what was actually going on down below in real time. His artistic skills left a lot to be desired. At school, he'd hated art with a passion. If he was honest, he'd hated all of school with a passion, but art particularly so. He not only wasn't any good; he also had never had the patience for it. Frustration had bubbled up and out as disruption at school. Here, that simply wasn't an option.

It was just as Liam was about to screw up his hand-drawn map in frustration and start again that he noticed a change in the movements below. And it was dramatic. Squeezing his eyes hard to push away the waves of tired-ness, he watched as a vehicle swung into the compound. He quickly snapped photographs of its arrival, then of the occupants exiting it and entering one of the buildings. This in itself had been a new development, but the one that followed it was immediately more worrying. Through the scope, Liam watched as a patrol of a dozen soldiers fanned out below them and started to head their way.

Shit . . .

Liam kept on with the scope, watching as the men moved slowly away from the farm buildings and up the hill towards their OP. For a moment he thought that perhaps it was just a routine check. They'd seen the soldiers carry out checks of the local area before. But this, Liam soon realized, was different. They weren't just taking a routine stroll to see if anything was up – they were walking with purpose, looking for something. And he could see that they were focused on what lay further up the hill.

He switched to the SLR, took some snaps, then was back on with the scope. The men, their fatigues giving no indication of their owner's loyalties, were clearly now making their way up the slope and showing no signs of changing direction or heading back to their base.

But why? Liam thought. What the hell had got them spooked enough after all this time to decide to take a stroll up towards them? Had they been compromised? And if so, how? He could think of no way that anything he or the others had done could have drawn attention to their presence.

Focusing now on getting as much INT as he could, Liam went back to the SLR. Making use of its hugely capable zoom lens, he moved from soldier to soldier, focusing in on their faces and quickly taking a rapid succession of portrait photographs. Their expressions were serious, determined. It was clear to him that they weren't messing around and were ready for a fight, should one kick off.

Liam quickly and quietly roused first Sergeant Biggs and then the others.

'What's up?' hissed the sergeant. Despite his chirpy West Country lilt, Biggs was solid and scarred, and looked like the only alcohol he ever drank was rocket propellant. With him came a ripe, warm stink and Liam almost gagged. He nodded to the sergeant to get himself up to the eyepiece of the spotting scope.

'Vehicle arrived fifteen minutes ago,' he reported. 'Then about two minutes ago, that—'

'Fuck . . .'

Cordner was now up, and alongside him was the final member of their four-man squad, a corporal called John Pearce who sounded like Sean Bean but didn't quite cut it in the looks department.

'Things about to get fruity?' asked Pearce.

'Looks that way,' Liam confirmed.

'Agreed,' said Biggs. 'And we need to be ready to get the hell out.'

'Any chance I can see the tour operator when we get back?' said Pearce. 'This holiday has been total and utter bollocks.'

'Wind your neck in,' said Biggs, and Pearce fell quiet.

Liam stared down the SLR. The soldiers were still only a couple of hundred metres or so up from the buildings, but their direction hadn't changed. Then one of them stopped and dropped to the ground, halting the others in the process.

The soldier rose, holding out what he had found on the ground.

Through the SLR the object glared at Liam, almost like it was laughing at him. His breath caught in his throat, but he forced his voice out regardless, croaking as he spoke.

'They've found a fucking ration bag!' he hissed through clenched teeth. 'They've found a fucking *ration bag*! We've been compromised!'

3

The last thing Liam saw through the viewfinder of the SLR before he stuffed it into its case was the patrol of soldiers climbing the hill, weapons now up and in the shoulder, and aiming them up the slope in the general direction of their position. They didn't know where Liam and the others were yet, but they soon would if they kept on moving. What had been a simple go look-see patrol had, on the finding of the empty ration bag, turned on a pin. The soldiers now knew someone was out there in the dark, and it was obvious that their clear intention was to eliminate the threat they posed. Liam knew they meant business.

Orders were barked and echoed round the trees, the soldiers now moving swiftly and in well-practised formation, using the trees as cover as they advanced in twos. As yet, no shots had been fired, but Liam had no doubt at all that it was only a matter of time.

'Where the fuck did that ration bag come from?' Pearce snarled, stuffing the last of his kit into his bergen like he was trying to punch a hole in it.

'At this moment, it doesn't fucking matter,' growled Biggs, the first of them to be ready for the off. 'What does, is that we scoot sharpish before those bastards are all over us like the kind of rash you've probably grown used to, Pearce. Understood?'

Liam clipped his own bergen shut, made a last check of his sleeping area and, satisfied that there was nothing left behind, was back to the sergeant and waiting instructions.

'Ready?'

Three stern voices answered Biggs with a simple 'Sarge.'

'We extract in two-by-twos,' said Biggs. 'Fire and manoeuvre all the way. No messing. No heroics. No fucking Rambo shite either. Understood?'

There was no answer. There didn't need to be.

'Scott, you and Cordner are out first. We'll cover you. As soon as you're topside, we'll lob in a few smoke grenades and flash bangs, anything to distract them, then put down some covering fire to keep their heads down.'

At that, Liam and Cordner edged forward, ready for the off. Liam's stomach was twisting itself tight as adrenaline coursed through him.

'We'll wait till you have cover and are slamming some rounds into them,' continued Biggs. 'Then we'll join you. From then on, you know the routine. Fire and manoeuvre all the way to the extraction point. We'll call it in on the way. Questions?'

There were none – if there had even been time. For now they all heard the voices. The enemy patrol was edging closer.

Liam, crouched next to Cordner, readied his weapon.

Sergeant Biggs lobbed two smoke grenades in quick succession from the rear exit of the OP, adding in a flash bang for good measure. Then, from the spy hole at the front, Pearce kicked off with a barrage of covering fire.

'Move!'

With Biggs's voice ringing in his ears, smoke swirling in the dark, and the hellish crack of automatic rifle fire snapping through the trees, Liam was up out of the hole. A few paces on he swung round to where the enemy were advancing, dropped down to one knee and opened fire. Short sharp bursts spat from his SA80, covering Cordner as the Irish man heaved himself up and out of the hole and raced past behind him. A few seconds later, Liam heard Cordner follow his example, giving it some with covering fire and yelling over to him to get moving.

Liam eased off the trigger, hammered himself up off

the cold earth and to his feet, and raced on. And so it continued, each of them providing covering fire as the other moved, until they were both clear of the scrape, and had enough cover from the scrub and trees around them to provide fire support for Biggs and Pearce.

More smoke grenades took to the air, a couple of flash-bangs, and Liam knew that Biggs and Pearce were on their way.

The air was thick with the sound of rifle fire mixing with shouts from the enemy soldiers, now desperate to get their quarry before it escaped.

Biggs and Pearce slid in behind them, faces determined and grim.

An explosion lit the night sky like a firework display.

'Reckon they've found the scrape,' said Biggs. 'Must have seriously pissed them off, eh? Let's move!'

As Liam and Cordner had been first out of the OP, it was the turn of Biggs and Pearce to take point, slipping off into the darkness as the other two continued with their covering fire. Then Liam and Cordner were on the move once more.

'Ready?' asked Cordner.

Liam lowered his weapon and was on his feet. 'Last one to the bar's a REMF,' he said, and he was off. Even if he was the youngest in the squad, if there was one thing he was never going to be, it was a rear echelon motherfucker.

Major Willis was standing behind his desk, glaring at Liam and the rest of the patrol. On the desk, in plain sight for them all to see, was the evidence from their OP that none of them wanted to take the blame for: the innocent-looking silver-foil food pouch.

The commanding officer had wasted no time in getting them all in front of him. They'd not even had time to change, and Liam was knackered and in desperate need of a shower.

'Well?'

Liam and the others remained quiet.

The major, who though the smallest in the room by noticeable inches had enough force of personality to fill a football stadium, raised his left eyebrow.

'To be frank, gentlemen,' he began, 'I am not entirely sure what stinks more: your pathetic, shit-covered carcasses, or that one of you managed to put your entire operation at risk by leaving a trace of your presence for the enemy to discover. Need I remind any of you that you are here because the army, in its apparent wisdom, seems to think that you are among its very finest and best? And that this' – the major picked up the foil food pouch from his desk and held it out in front of them –

'well, it's not exactly showing you at your best in any shape or form now, is it? You are supposed to be in intelligence. You are supposed to be invisible. Recce Platoon is supposed to be the ears and the eyes of the battalion. Good intelligence means the right men and the right weapon system deployed for the situation. Bad or half-baked intelligence means a full-on shit storm. Without accurate, current intelligence a soldier, a platoon, an army is blind. And if you can't get intelligence without being discovered, you are no good to us.'

Major Willis was still standing holding the food pouch.

'I am inclined to suggest,' he said, his voice quiet, 'that it would be good form on your part if one of you at least stepped forward and took this out of my hands.'

Biggs was the one to take the pouch, but Liam knew the mistake had not been his. He felt sick. What if it was one of *his* pouches? The truth was that he couldn't be sure it hadn't come from his bag. He couldn't remember checking. He'd been so focused on taking pictures and trying to draw maps.

'I will say no more,' Major Willis said, sitting back in his chair and resting his hands clasped together in his lap, 'but one of you buggered this up good and proper. Which is a shame because, by all accounts, your subsurface observation exercise was going rather well. The INT collected was top-notch, and even the map drawing wasn't a total loss, but from here on in this kind of sloppiness never occurs again. Do you understand?'

Liam joined in with a 'Yes, sir.'

'The Light Reconnaissance Commanders Course is tough. It's meant to be. If it was easy, any fucker could do it, and what would be the point of that?'

Liam was only partly listening. What he really wanted to do was hightail it out of there and go through his kit. Why hadn't he checked and double-checked everything? If the pouch was his, he'd never forgive himself. As for Biggs, Cordner and Pearce, he didn't dare think what they'd all have to say to him.

'Now bugger off, the lot of you, and for the love of God have a shower before some jobsworth comes in and decides we've secretly developed a new kind of biological weapon!'

Liam stared at his kit, all laid out neatly in front of him on the floor of his room.

'Bollocks . . .'

He'd now been through every pocket, every fold of cloth, every single nook and cranny in his clothes, webbing and bergen, but the evidence was clear: the food pouch that had screwed them over was his. He was one down, the space where it should be amongst the others glaring at him like an open wound.

Liam crouched down to check his bergen once again, even though he knew it was pointless, that there was no missing food pouch somehow still hidden inside, waiting to clear him from all accusation and prove his innocence.

As he dragged the bergen towards him, a pair of boots appeared at the door.

'So it was you with the missing food pouch in the stinking damp scrape, was it?'

Liam didn't laugh because it wasn't funny. Not to him anyway.

'Fuck off, Pearce,' he said.

'Could've been any one of us,' Pearce replied. 'Just turns out that this time you're wanker of the week. Well done. Want me to get you a special badge?'

'You're not the one who put the whole OP to shit,' said Liam. 'What if we'd been out for real? What then, eh? Wouldn't be so fucking hysterical if we'd all got our faces shot off because I couldn't keep my personal admin in order, would it?'

'Our exit was perfect,' said Pearce. 'From the smoke grenades and flash-bangs to the fire manoeuvre. And you know what, you did us a favour.'

'How so?'

'If it hadn't been for you being a bit shit, then we'd never had been given the chance to carry out a response to a threat as we did. It's always good to enjoy a bit of a firefight.'

Two further pairs of boots arrived.

'Well, my dear Watson,' said Cordner, 'do we have a suspect?'

'Scott's guilty as charged,' said Pearce. 'The evidence is right here in front of him. Or not, I suppose.'

Cordner and Biggs laughed.

'Well,' said Biggs. 'Looks like you earned yourself a nickname. I'm going with Ration Bag – or RB for short, if you want.'

Pearce nodded, Cordner applauded. Liam attempted a smile. But he couldn't keep it there for long.

'Cordner and Pearce, you two, fuck off now and have a shower – you smell like you've been shat out of a cow's arse,' said Biggs. He stood for a moment watching Liam in silence. 'So how long are you planning on keeping up with this bollocks, then?' he asked as soon as he and Liam were alone. 'If you can't deal with a mistake and learn from it, you're fucked. You know that.'

'It was my fault,' said Liam, still unable to pull himself out of the black mood draped over him like a funeral cloak. 'I fucked up. I could have got us all killed.'

'Mate, we've all fucked up. Soldiering isn't exactly all easy-peasy now, is it?'

Easy-peasy? thought Liam. Had Biggs really just said that? He stood up, turning his back on his kit, and sat on the edge of his bed.

'So,' continued Biggs, 'log this and move on. Mistakes are how we learn. From here on in, no fucker is going to come close to you when it comes to being on top of their own kit now, are they?'

'Totally,' Liam said. 'Thanks.'

'And remember,' said Biggs, standing up, 'we've the CFT coming up next. You may be fit, but you need to smash your personal best. So get some rest. Immediately.'

The morning of the Combat Fitness Test arrived, cold but bright. Liam was with the rest of the LRCC lads at the starting line dressed in his battle kit, which weighed in at over twenty pounds. It didn't sound much, but running with it was no easy task.

Liam had been training hard for the course and had already got his eight-mile CFT time down from two hours to one hour twenty. Today his time was going to be even better. He knew the course backwards. Tracks over open heathland first. Then up into the hills with a couple of sharp climbs. And then back down through woodland. He could nail it. And he wasn't going to let the screw-up yesterday put him off.

'Right, lads,' said Sergeant Welsh, one of the physical training instructors and a force to be reckoned with, both in size and ability. 'You know what you have to do today. You're all fit, you're all ready for this. So get out there and prove it. Just remember to take in enough water – I don't want anyone forgetting what they're doing and ending up in a state because of dehydration. Understood?'

As one, Liam and the others answered with a clear, loud 'Yes, Sergeant!'

For a moment the air was still, the only sound that of soldiers sucking as much oxygen as they could down into their lungs, readying themselves for what they all knew was going to be a proper ballbreaker of a run.

Liam replayed in his mind the moment he'd seen the soldier stand up holding the ration bag. Not today, he thought. This was going to be his moment and he was going to burn any memory of that cock-up to ash by the end of it.

The shallow crack of a starting pistol broke the tension and the mass of soldiers took off, charging past the PTI, their singular aim to get to the end of the next eight miles as quickly as possible, no matter what.

Liam, jostled by those around him, fought to keep his

footing. No one was out to deliberately trip anyone else up, but neither were they there to do each other any favours. The CFT was every soldier for himself, and Liam elbowed his way forwards too.

Soon the pack thinned, as much to allow people to breathe as anything else. Liam focused on his breathing, keeping it regular, with two sharp inhales through his nose followed by a single exhale from his mouth. He'd learned while reading up on fitness and running that this forced the lungs to take in more oxygen.

The route was marked, so all Liam had to do was keep an eye out ahead for where he was going and concentrate on pushing himself through the pain.

'*Pain is weakness leaving the body . . .*' It was a mantra jokingly bandied about, but it rang true. If you couldn't push through the pain and keep going, then there was no way you were ever going to make it.

Two miles in and the inclining track Liam was now following was becoming gradually steeper. He wasn't at the back of the pack, but he also wasn't at the front, not yet anyway. He was keeping a fast but steady pace, ensuring that as the final miles came in he would have enough left to up a gear and really go for it. Once he passed the halfway point, that's exactly what he would do.

The track was winding up a slope, a snake crawling

its way slowly up a mountainside. Then it snapped itself over a false horizon and Liam was heading back down, feet pounding hard as he accelerated.

The four-mile marker zipped past. The sun was climbing and it was getting hotter. In his mind, Liam dropped a gear and floored it. Upping his pace, he thundered past three other soldiers. One of them was Pearce, but he didn't make eye contact or throw in a comment. This wasn't the time.

Ahead, Liam caught sight of Cordner. The wiry Irish bastard had the build of a cross-country runner and was flying along at a hell of a pace. Liam knew that passing him would be a task in itself, but at least he could use Cordner as a marker to keep pace with. So that's what he focused on now. With three miles left to go, his personal best was in reach. He was sweating.

It was as the route dipped into some thick woodland that Liam started to feel strange. He was beyond tired now, mining deep into what reserves he had left. His legs were on automatic, keeping going despite feeling like jelly. His feet were no longer landing with control, had seemed to gain weight, like they were now made of lead. Sunlight was flickering through the trees.

Liam shook his head, squeezing his eyes tight to combat a dizziness that was starting to swirl forward from the back of his brain. He had to keep going.

Stopping was not an option. But what the hell was wrong?

Had he taken in enough water? He wasn't sure. Yes, he'd sipped from his bottle, he was sure of it, but not too much – he didn't want cramp. He'd have some more in a minute.

Liam's left foot caught on a tree root sticking out of the middle of the track. He tripped, jarring his right leg as he caught himself, carried on.

Ahead, Cordner was edging away. That wasn't a problem. The bloke was a gazelle. Liam had never even considered catching him up.

A puddle came up fast and he leaped over it rather than risk any stones and rocks hidden beneath the surface. But his landing was off and his knees went this time, dropping him to the ground.

Liam hit the dirt hard, sharp daggers of pain stabbing him. But he was up again, on his feet, pushing forward. It wasn't far to go now, he was sure of it.

Keep going, I've just got to keep going . . . come on . . . fucking well move it!

Another tree root, but Liam had spotted it early enough to dodge it, and he zipped past.

Nausea then came at him, a great wave of it sweeping over him, and his head spun.

Keep going . . .

Liam saw flashes of light dancing across his vision. He shook his head, only a little too much, and dizziness grabbed him.

Must . . . keep . . .

He didn't see the dip ahead, hit the deck before he could do anything to stop himself.

Darkness.

4

'You total fucking idiot.'

Liam, lying on a bed in the medical centre with a drip jabbed into his arm, was in no mood for a bollocking. Not that he could do anything about the fact that he was going to get one.

'Dehydration!' continued Sergeant Welsh, voice dripping with disbelief and disdain. 'What in the name of Christ were you thinking? Oh, you weren't, were you? Fucksake, Scott. Are you intent on getting binned? Because, believe me, that kind of shit is exactly what'll make it happen.'

Liam kept his mouth shut. He was too pissed off with himself to reply.

'You're one of the fastest, fittest blokes here, and you go and make a schoolboy error like that? You ran that like you were intent on self-destruction.'

'I'd been taking in water,' said Liam.

The sergeant chucked a water bottle to Liam. 'This is yours. You'll notice it's pretty fucking full.'

Liam reached for the bottle. He was sure he'd drunk enough. But the weight of the thing proved otherwise.

'What happened on the surveillance exercise I can understand and forgive,' said the sergeant. 'But this?' He leaned forward. The look on his face was stern enough to stop time. 'Soldiers die from dehydration,' he said. 'You know that. Holy fuck, Scott, it even makes head-line news!'

Yeah, it does, thought Liam. But I'm not dead, am I, so why don't you fuck off and leave me alone?

'It's one of the first things you learn! Drink water. Stay hydrated. It's not just about keeping your body working, but your head. Dehydration out in theatre? That leads to poor judgement, bad decisions, and soldiers – not just you – getting slotted.'

'I know . . .'

'Certainly doesn't fucking well seem like it to me.' The sergeant fell quiet.

Liam didn't even attempt to fill the silence. He had more than enough reason to believe the sergeant would chew and spit out any of his words.

'Right,' Sergeant Welsh said at last. 'Know this, Scott – I've dropped soldiers for less than what you did today. They've been out on their arse, told to come back when they're ready. But with you, I'm going to make an exception.'

'Thanks, Sergeant,' said Liam.

'Don't thank me,' Welsh replied. 'And I warn you here and now – do not make me regret it. I know your reputation. You've more than proved your worth in theatre. Frankly, though, I don't give a flying fuck about any of that. It's given me reason to hold off on throwing you back to your battalion, but nothing else. From here on in, you need to sort your head out and get with the programme. You got me?'

Liam nodded.

'Last chance saloon,' said the sergeant, standing up and moving away from Liam's bed. 'This time you stay. Next time, I'll personally ensure my boot print tattoos your arse deep enough that you'll be wearing a memory of me for fucking years.'

And with that he was gone.

Liam leaned back on the bed. He'd just got off lightly and the relief he felt didn't mix too well with the knowledge of what an idiot he was being. It was down to him whether he stayed or not. No one else was in control of it. If he kept on like this he would be the cause of his own downfall. And that, he knew, was unacceptable on every level.

It was time for a proper one-to-one with himself.

And the only way to do that was with someone else.

Clint Eastwood, Liam's old mate from 4 Rifles, was the only person Liam felt he could talk to. He phoned him as soon as he was discharged from the medical centre. They'd served together in Afghanistan and balding, smiling, forty-something Clint – aka Cowboy – had always been someone he had trusted. He'd insisted on buying Liam breakfast. Liam wasn't sure which was greasier, the floor or the plate of food in front of him.

'Now this is living, hey, Scott?'

'Do you think they deep fry everything?' Liam asked, staring at his breakfast. It was so large he was surprised the rickety table they were sitting at could handle two such meals at once.

Clint raised his pint mug of tea. 'Judging by this mug, I reckon so,' he said, and took a gulp.

The café sat in a parking area alongside a road not too far from where Liam was training. It was, at best, functional, though judging by the damp patches on the walls it wouldn't be long before the place simply gave up and sank into the ground.

'How's life?' Liam asked. 'How are the kids?'

It had been a while since Liam had met up with Clint. After Afghanistan, life in 4 Rifles – their battalion – had led them in different directions. Clint had left the battalion; he was back home with his family and had returned to the Army Reserve. He also had a good business running self-defence classes. They saw little of each other. But he was still the person Liam most trusted. The basic self-defence moves Clint had taught him when he was a rookie out in Camp Bastion had saved his life. And Liam would never forget it.

Clint grinned. Something he did a lot. He was one irritatingly happy bastard. 'Everything's mint, mate,' he said.

'And the business?'

'Rock-and-roll awesome,' Clint answered. 'Now cut to the chase – what's up?'

'I'm not sure about the LRCC,' Liam said. 'That's it, really.'

'Rubbish,' said Clint. 'You're made for it, mate. What's your bone with it? You were smart to work out that the most powerful weapon now is not just the gun with the biggest bang or the longest range. It's intelligence. And if you can make it in Recce Platoon, maybe one day you can try out for the SAS. Don't tell me you wouldn't want to.'

Liam shovelled some black pudding into his mouth. It was crisp on the outside, soft on the inside, and totally delicious.

'I fucked up twice,' he said. 'Once on a subsurface surveillance op, and then on the CFT.'

'So?'

'So I'm beginning to think I lucked out on this one. Wondering if I'd be better heading back to 4 Rifles and getting my lance-corporal experience up to speed.'

Clint was already halfway through his meal, eating it like he was afraid someone was going to steal it.

'Hungry?'

'Always,' said Clint. 'And I'll be sweating this off later anyway.'

Of that Liam had no doubt. Clint had been the oldest of the lads out with him in Afghanistan. But he'd also been the fittest.

'But don't go changing the subject,' continued Clint. 'You're not a quitter, mate. You messed up. The ration pouch? That stuff happens. Job done. The dehydration? If we weren't in this café, I'd give you a slap. You know better.' He drained his mug of tea, asked for another. 'I've seen you do what you do. I've seen you react under fire. Mate, I've been under your command, remember? The battalion wouldn't have supported your application for the LRCC if the powers that be didn't think you were up to it. You are. So move on, move up. Simple.'

Liam said, 'You know my lance-corporal experience

won't count for shit if I pass and get into Recce Platoon, right?'

Clint shrugged. 'So what?'

'Good point.'

'I'm serious,' said Clint. 'What does that matter? You will have the rank – you just won't be in a command role for a while. Hardly a deal-breaker when you consider the fact that you will be doing a job few others are cut out for. And that's worth more, I reckon, don't you?'

Liam nodded and finished the last of his breakfast.

'You're a good soldier, Liam,' said Clint, now halfway through his second mug of tea. 'Better than good. And unless I'm mistaken – and I know I'm not – you're in this for the duration, right? So suck it up and crack on. If you don't – I'll kick your arse . . .'

The memory of Clint's voice faded away as Liam forced himself back to his present-day reality. Here he was in an interrogation room getting his arse kicked by a different bastard and he had to work out how to get through it. It was no time to think about the past. He started to go through again, detail by detail, everything he had learned about surviving capture. One thing he could do was focus on his training, try to force his brain to remember the basics, like how to strip his rifle. He was in the process of putting the weapon back

together in his mind when the hood was ripped from
his head.

'Name.'

Liam's eyes were blurry but he now recognized the
voice. It was Sergeant Welsh.

'Scott, Liam . . .' Liam replied.

'So how do you feel now that you know you've fucked
up for the last time?'

Liam was beyond thinking of a response and the
question just bounced off him. 'Scott, Liam . . .' He was
on autopilot, couldn't say anything else even if he
wanted to.

'You can stop with all that bollocks,' said the
sergeant. 'I said I'd throw you out if you fucked up one
more time, didn't I? Well, this is that time, Scott. It's
time to say goodbye, and frankly, I'm pleased.'

'Scott, Liam . . .'

The sergeant was out of his seat now and round to
Liam's side, speaking quietly into his left ear. 'You
haven't got what it takes, Scott,' he whispered. 'We've
pushed you and you've crumbled. No more fucking
around. You're leaving this room as someone who can't
hack what Recce Platoon is all about. And about time.
Last thing we need is some dick with a couple of medals
thinking he's the hero. You hear me? We want you to
fuck off!'

Liam kept quiet, but stood his ground.

Sergeant Welsh leaned in real close. Liam could feel the man's breath against his ear.

'You've failed, Scott,' he said. 'Totally. Fucking. Failed.'

5

'You really don't get it, do you?' said the sergeant, returning to his chair and opening a drawer. 'You've
done your two tours, you've proved yourself as a regular
soldier, a decent one – just not good enough for what
Recce Platoon is after.'

'Scott, Liam . . .' said Liam. If he'd failed, then they'd
have to drag him from there because he wasn't quitting,
not ever. He'd come too far, gone through too much.
Despite his exhaustion, he stood firm.

The sergeant stared hard at Liam, a hawk eying its
prey. 'You see, this is what I mean, Scott,' he said, leaning forward. 'You're arrogant! You really think that just
because you've fired a couple of RPGs in 'Stan you can
waltz into this and everything's fine and dandy. Well,
here's a wake-up call, kid: it fucking well isn't. Go back
to the infantry – you're not wanted here.'

Welsh had to just be playing mind games with him,

thought Liam. If he had failed, they'd have dragged him out by now, surely. Which meant that once this was over, it would be stress positions and icy water yet again. But he was numb to it now, couldn't feel anything, think straight. They could beat the crap out of him for all he cared; he wasn't quitting.

The sergeant stood up from his desk. Liam's eyes came back into focus and he watched as Welsh approached him again. But this time, Liam noticed immediately that something was different. For a few seconds he couldn't work out what it was, his brain running idiotically slow.

Then it clicked: the sergeant was wearing a black band round his left arm, just above the elbow. Why? What was that about? Was there a funeral? What the hell were they going to do to him now? A mock execution? He wasn't sure how much more he could take, and a blindfold and a gun against his head might just tip him over the edge. Somehow he had to remain strong, no matter what. Just had to.

'Well?' asked the sergeant. 'You have anything else you want to say?'

But that band bothered Liam. He knew that it was significant. Hadn't something been mentioned about it during the briefing before the exercise? But what the hell was it? Then, as the sergeant came to stand right next to him again, he remembered. It was a sign, wasn't it? Yes, that was it, a sign that something was over. But what?

'You've passed, Scott,' the sergeant said. 'Well done.'

Then something clicked in Liam's mind. The band – it meant the exercise was finished. It was a visual signal that would only be used when the interrogation was over.

'Scott, Liam . . .' he said, unable to get his thoughts straight.

'We know who you are, Scott,' said Welsh, a hint of a smile creeping across his face. 'You've passed. The exercise is over. Well done!'

Liam couldn't think, couldn't speak. He'd passed. He'd fucking well passed! It was over. He'd survived the interrogation, the torture. He'd done it!

The elation was overwhelming and it took all of Liam's will power to stop himself from collapsing to the floor with relief.

'Seriously? We're done?'

Sergeant Welsh nodded. 'Now fuck off will you, Scott? You look like shit.'

Two months later, Liam stood in the briefing room. It was the perfect example of military simplicity: tables, chairs, a whiteboard, and that was it. Comfort was not a consideration. Functionality ruled.

The whole of Liam's platoon was there, approximately thirty men, all of them reconnaissance soldiers. And he was not only one of the least experienced, but also of the lowest rank, a lance corporal being the bottom rank for an NCO.

'I bet this is where we find out that Recce Platoon is actually responsible for the sodding laundry and latrines,' grumbled Pearce.

Liam laughed. Since completing the LRCC, life seemed to have passed in a blur. He could recall snatches of it, but it was all so jumbled up he wasn't quite sure what had happened when. The training had been intense, exciting, stressful, exhausting and at times downright terrifying – particularly the escape and evasion exercise – but despite his initial misgivings about whether or not he had made the right decision, he'd completed it. Since then, having joined the Recce Platoon back at his battalion, they had been kept busy on numerous training exercises, all designed to hone the skills they had learned, and give them new ones. His feet had barely touched the ground.

An officer strode to the front of the room, walking with purpose.

Captain Owusu was in his early thirties. Tanzanian by birth, but brought to the UK as an infant by his parents, his accent was part African home life, part Brixton, all overlaid by British army officer speak. Average height, but not average build, he spent his spare time chasing adrenaline by skydiving, mountain biking, surfing – indeed, doing any sport that had the word 'extreme' in the description. His only mode of transport was a weary Transit van, the white paint of which was fighting a losing battle with the rust it tried to hide. The captain couldn't care less that it was an eyesore in the car park. As far as he was concerned, it held all his kit, and that was what he cared about. The captain, like most officers, had a reputation for not just keeping up with his men, but bettering them – Captain Owusu wasn't the kind of person who would ever ask anyone to do something if he couldn't do it himself.

Liam and the others fell silent. This was no ordinary briefing and the atmosphere was thick with anticipation.

'Good afternoon, gentlemen. Firstly, thank you all for taking time out from your busy schedules to be here. I promise I won't keep you for long.'

A rattle of laughter skipped around the room. Liam, like everyone else, knew that the meeting wasn't optional.

'In two weeks the battalion will be deployed to Kenya,' said the captain. 'This is a routine six-week exercise at the British Army Training Unit in Kenya, called BATUK for short.'

So far nothing new, thought Liam. So why had they been called in specially?

'As I'm sure you are all aware,' continued Owusu, 'the local troops – the Kenyan Defence Force – have a job on to deal with the threat of the terrorist group Al Shabaab. Our task, as the battalion's Recce Platoon, is to go out there and help them. While everyone else at BATUK will be taking part in training and live-fire exercises, we will be teaching the KDF the kinds of skills that I hope each of you is now expert in.'

Al Shabaab. Liam had seen the name cropping up now and again in the press. The militant group was a serious threat, linked to a slew of horrific attacks.

'I will now hand over to Lieutenant Young, who will give you a quick recap on exactly who the Kenyans are dealing with.'

Lieutenant Young took the floor. He was the polar opposite of the captain, all height, blond hair and public school upbringing. And yet, like Owusu, he spoke simply and directly. Liam had heard that Young's parents had wanted him to become a lawyer and had been none too impressed when, after graduating, he had gone straight off to Sandhurst.

'Al Shabaab, as I am sure you are all aware, is an affiliate of Al Qaeda. Based in Somalia, it is fighting an insurgency against the recognized Somali federal government, based in Mogadishu.'

Now that was a name Liam knew, thanks in no small part to the movie *Black Hawk Down*. Based on the Battle of Mogadishu, it gave a graphic, if not entirely accurate, account of the United States' attempt to capture a Somalian warlord called Mohamed Farrah Aidid.

'Due to the group's capacity to carry out attacks beyond its borders, notably in Kenya itself,' said the lieutenant, 'anything we can do to help the KDF not only prepare for attacks, but also prevent them being carried out in the first place, is vital. The Ethiopian military is doing the same – there is a concerted regional effort to stop the terrorists.'

Liam remembered his last tour of Afghanistan. He had gone up close and personal with the Taliban. He had no doubt that this new enemy was just as capable and ruthless.

'The group,' continued Young, 'has targeted peace-keepers, civilians and the military, and it seems to be showing no signs of backing down or easing off. It has a strong influence on the ground; its leaders are all members of a Shura Council. This council has not only put together its own policy for Somalia, it also fully expects local administrations to abide by it.'

When Liam had first heard about the training exercise, he had been expecting something in line with what he had been used to as a regular soldier in 2 Rifles – some kind of activity that involved all of them working together to learn and become better soldiers. Here, though, in Recce Platoon, it was something different. Instead of focusing only on themselves, they were heading out to aid others. And he liked the sound of that.

The lieutenant sat down and Captain Owusu was at the front once again.

'The KDF is building up to going on the offensive,' he said. 'Following recent events in the capital involving Al Shabaab, the government there has decided against simply preparing for another attack. Instead, it wants to deploy into Somalia to deal with the terrorists there before they even have a chance to cross the border. And that is where we come in.'

Liam was listening intently now and he leaned forward to make sure he didn't miss a single word.

'Information is key to this, and our mission is to ensure that we teach the Kenyans how to be proper sneaky bastards.'

This got a laugh, but the captain's face didn't move.

'If the Kenyans can establish exactly what Al Shabaab is up to, where it is located, and anything else deemed important, then it has a much higher chance of success than simply going in hoping for the best. So, needless to say, I will be depending on all of you not just to demonstrate your professionalism, but to do so with a skill set that will allow us to arm the KDF with exactly what they need to carry out their role and face down the threat of Al Shabaab effectively. Any questions?'

No one raised a hand.

'Good,' said the captain. 'So let's all get a shift on and ready ourselves. Dismissed!'

Two weeks after their initial briefing, Liam and the rest of his platoon were flown to the Kenyan capital, Nairobi. From there, it was a 200km hop north by helicopter to BATUK in Nanyuki. And the flight was almost over.

Liam was strapped into the back of the Chinook. It had been bumpy and noisy, but that hadn't made it any less awesome. Around him sat other soldiers from the platoon, their kit piled up between them. Now they were coming in to land.

Liam did his best not to smile, but it was almost impossible. He had done some amazing things in his army life, but all as a regular soldier. Now, though, as the Chinook touched down, the ramp dropped open, and swirls of dust danced up to greet them, he was part of an elite group. This was where he was meant to be: a new life, a new experience and, now, a new enemy . . .

6

'Not a bad place for a holiday,' said Cordner, as Liam followed him into where their eight-man section would be bunking down together at BATUK. 'Wonder what the room service is like?'

It was late afternoon and the fierce heat of Kenya was a shock to the system after life in the UK. The air was bone dry and the temperature had been enough to start him sweating almost immediately. To Liam, it was like he'd fallen asleep en route and woken up back in Camp Bastion in Afghanistan, and the time that had passed since his last tour had been nothing but a dream.

Bastion had housed approximately 28,000 people and was the size of a large town. BATUK was considerably smaller, but nonetheless had a familiar feel to it. This was in part due to the landscape. Though visibly greener in places than the Afghan desert, with nearby craggy hills displaying thick foliage, it was similarly hot and dusty. The snow-capped Mount Kenya was visible in the distance, clouds hanging thick around it like damp towels.

It was why, six times a year, the British Army sent soldiers out here to train. The army had a specially-designed Afghan village somewhere in the forests of Norfolk, but for soldiers being sent to theatre in hot countries BATUK provided a more realistic training environment. Surrounded by a bombproof wall built of Hescos – huge canvas bags filled with sand, grit and soil dug up from the surrounding area – the camp included a hospital, helicopter landing area, gym and mess hall. It really was a mini version of the UK's presence in Afghanistan.

The accommodation, however, wasn't quite up to Bastion standard. Green canvas tents, going grey in the sun, housed the constantly rotating groups of soldiers from the UK. A small, dusty parade ground was flanked by an area hung with lines to dry clothing and doss bags. And if the wind was heading in the wrong direction, the distinct whiff of chemical toilets would drift by.

Their section included Biggs, Pearce and Cordner. Liam had only really got to know the other four in the eight-man section since joining the Recce Platoon proper after completing the LRCC. Over the next six weeks they'd be living in each other's pockets, so he hoped they'd all get on. One of the platoon, Callum Waterman, was already settled in and Liam nodded a hello; they had spent some time together before the flight out.

'Home sweet home, hey?' said Waterman. 'You've not been out here before, have you?'

Liam shook his head as he started to sort through his kit. Making anywhere, even a hole in the ground, feel like home was something all soldiers did. Usually a few family photographs would appear, a poster or two, some random souvenirs. Liam's photographs were not of his family, but of some of the lads he'd served with during his past two tours. He had little contact with his parents: his father was a total tosser, and his mum, though proud of what Liam had gone on to achieve, was rarely in touch.

'Finished my LRCC a few weeks back,' said Liam. 'Before that I did two tours in Afghanistan. So this is a first. Reminds me of Bastion.'

A distant sound caught him off guard. It was a strange howling noise that set the hairs on his neck on end.

'That's the great thing about coming out here,' said Waterman. 'You get a free safari trip thrown in!'

'What the hell was that?' Liam asked. The sound had reminded him of a school trip to a zoo when he was a kid.

'Hyena,' said Waterman. 'Get used to it. The wildlife out here is as beautiful as it is dangerous. And most of it wants to try and eat you.'

Waterman was a corporal, and as far as Liam had so far gathered he had only two interests: heavy metal music and horror. If he wasn't listening to one then he was watching or reading the other. He had a fair number of tattoos too; whereas Liam had just the one – the Rifles insignia on his left arm – Waterman clearly viewed his skin as a canvas, somehow just keeping it in check enough not to annoy the army. He'd once given Liam a guided tour. It had been like a trip on a ghost train, with most of the tattoos representing some horror icon or another.

'I've been to worse places,' Waterman continued. 'The bar is out of bounds to non-permanent staff, but unless you're a complete alcoholic then you should be able to handle that, right?'

'A beer goes well in the heat, though,' said Liam, remembering thirsting after one in Afghanistan on more than one occasion.

'And at least we get to do decent stuff with our time out here rather than just playing at soldiering,' added Waterman. 'That's half the reason I went Recce. Got a bit tired of just training exercises out here – figured there was more to do than that, so here I am.'

Liam hoped Waterman was right about everything he'd said; he liked to stay busy. And although he was sure he'd dealt with his self-doubts, now and again he still wondered if joining Recce had been the right decision. Time would tell, he thought, and six weeks here was undoubtedly just what he needed.

Three other lads bumbled into the sleeping area to join them. Like Waterman, they were experienced Recce Platoon soldiers and clearly knew each other well, launching straight into handshakes and swearing and man-hugs. They were followed by Pearce, who immediately clocked the photographs Liam had put up.

'That taken during your last tour?'

The picture Pearce was referring to was of Liam standing with another soldier. They were both tanned, dusty, weighed down with kit, and beaming the grins of two lads happy in the moment.

'My first,' said Liam, unpacking his bergen. 'That's Cameron, good mate from Harrogate and Catterick. He didn't come home.'

'Sorry to hear that, mate,' said Pearce. 'That's properly shit.'

There was no fake mourning or awkwardness in Pearce's response, and Liam appreciated that. What he'd said was straight to the point and honest. A soldier talking.

'Mortar round got him. He was a bloody excellent soldier. Messed me up a bit, losing him.'

'I lost a mate too,' said Pearce. 'Fucking sniper slotted him while we were doing a foot patrol. Never found the bastard, either.'

For a moment, neither of them spoke. Then Biggs and Cordner were with them.

'Ah, crap,' said Cordner as he and Biggs wandered in and lobbed their own kit onto the two beds opposite Liam and Pearce. 'Is there nothing I can do to get away from you two shitheads?'

'Admit it,' Pearce replied. 'You requested to be with us. Couldn't live without a little midnight cuddle from RB.' He chuckled at his own joke and Liam grinned; his mate never missed the opportunity to take the piss out of him over the ration bag incident.

'Not much point trying to settle in straight away – we're all wanted in the briefing room sharpish,' Biggs said.

Liam hadn't forgotten about the briefing – he just wanted to make the most of whatever time he had, and settling in was important. Seeing the photograph of Cameron had reaffirmed his view that joining Recce Platoon had been a good decision. He had seen up close and personal just how fragile life was. Cameron's death had made him realize that he had to make the best of everything that came his way. It was why he'd managed to somehow get a transfer from 2 Rifles to 4 Rifles on returning from his first tour, so that he could get back out into theatre as quickly as possible. It was also why he'd gone for the LRCC.

Lieutenant Young popped his head into the sleeping area. 'Get a shift on, lads. Briefing in a couple of minutes.'

Everyone chorused a 'Yes, sir.'

Liam stopped unpacking and walked to the door. 'Best get going then. Bag ourselves some good seats.'

Pearce, Cordner and Biggs followed him out and soon they were all sitting with the rest of the Recce Platoon in a canvas-walled room, the canvas pulled tight against the elements around a steel frame. Behind them sat Waterman and the others from their section.

Captain Owusu was at the front waiting for the last of the soldiers to troop in. When they were all present and correct, an expectant silence fell.

The captain welcomed everyone then went straight into the reason they had all been called together.

'Tomorrow will be Day Two of your six weeks here in BATUK. As you can see, the weather is certainly better than back home. And the only cats you'll see walking around are big enough to bite your head off. But this is no holiday.'

Pearce leaned over to Liam. 'It's the last time I let you book online, mate,' he whispered. 'I specifically asked for two weeks getting pissed on a beach and you bring us here. What a twat.'

Liam didn't reply as Captain Owusu continued with his briefing.

'We are here to work, and to help the Kenyans as much as we can. Understood? Good.' The captain gave no pause for agreement. 'So that you are aware, you must all remain vigilant against insider attacks. Though the threat may not be as acute as that faced by most of you while in theatre, it is still very real and immediate.'

Afghanistan was a war zone, but Kenya, as far as Liam knew, wasn't. Threat to life had been an everyday occurrence while on tour, and even Camp Bastion hadn't been completely safe. Following a mortar attack by Taliban insurgents on the camp, he'd ended up in the hospital, luckily only with concussion. But BATUK? This was something he hadn't even considered.

Captain Owusu pinned photographs of five Kenyan soldiers on the wall behind him. The men all looked young, around the same age as Liam. Not only that, they didn't look like the kind of lads who would be easily persuaded to do something they didn't want to.

'Only three weeks ago,' Owusu continued, 'BATUK

was attacked by Al Shabaab terrorists. Seven Kenyan soldiers were injured, three seriously. Al Shabaab, it seems, is not content with just playing games in Somalia, and is now making serious inroads into Kenya itself. And it isn't about to back down without a serious and sustained rebuttal from the KDF.'

Liam wanted to know exactly what kind of attack had been carried out. Was it a suicide bomb or a coordinated ground assault? BATUK, like Bastion, seemed pretty impregnable.

'Not only that,' said that captain, interrupting Liam's thoughts, 'but following the attack, it was discovered that a number of the Kenyan soldiers had gone missing, presumably kidnapped.'

With a sick feeling, Liam knew immediately that these were the soldiers in the photographs.

'Al Shabaab is organized and ruthless. On that particular day, one terrorist who had managed to in-filtrate the camp and secure a job working in the mess blew himself up. At exactly the same time, BATUK was attacked at two other points. It was during this that these five men were taken.'

Liam was shocked. A suicide bomb was one thing, but to use such an attack as a distraction to snatch hostages was something else. And he didn't like the sound of it at all. No one did. IEDs terrified all soldiers, but you got on with the job and hoped you were lucky. Being taken hostage was another thing entirely. And, deep down, Liam felt — as did every other soldier he knew — that it would be better to be killed outright than end up in the hands of terrorists and at the mercy of their video cameras and sharp knives.

'Suffice to say,' said Captain Owusu, 'the camp is on high alert. So don't get lazy just because the sun's out and you're not back home in the pissing wet. Is that clear?'

'Sir,' said Liam, joining in with the rest of the platoon.

'Now get back to sorting out your kit. Tomorrow we start. Dismissed.'

Breakfast, as with every army breakfast Liam had ever had, was full of choice. It was as if those in charge of catering understood that not providing a full English would potentially result in mutiny. But if he was honest, Liam had never had much to complain about when it came to the food. Hell, even the ration packs were decent. There was a reason behind so much food being on offer, and that was simply the fact that soldiers burned calories — a lot of them. It wasn't unusual, on a hard day out training, for a soldier to need over 4000 calories just to get by. Today, though, Liam hadn't been tempted by the vast piles of bacon, egg, sausage, beans, mushrooms, black pudding, tomatoes and hash browns.

The heat didn't yet mix it too well with the grease, so he'd gone for a double helping of porridge with a couple of bananas and a few slices of toast and marmalade, all washed down with a decent brew.

With the most important meal of the day out of the way, they had then all been informed that the next few days were to be spent getting to know each other. No one had taken that seriously – soldiers, Liam knew, had a knack of getting to know each other within minutes of meeting. It was all part of being able to depend on each other in a life-or-death situation. No, the aim here was to ensure that the sections were working well together before getting involved with the Kenyans. It would also serve as a bit of revision.

Marching out from BATUK that morning had given Liam a better idea of what lay outside the camp's perimeter. It wasn't the Serengeti, but neither was it the Brecon Beacons. The green of vegetation stood out bright and lush against the red clay soil. Baobab trees, strange things that looked almost as though they'd been planted the wrong way up, their roots stretching for the sky, were dotted everywhere. A herd of zebra grazed in the distance.

Evidence of small-scale farming was all around them, from strips of land growing crops to wandering flocks of goats. He saw small huts assembled from scavenged materials: old doors, wattle and daub, dry wood and sheets of polythene. But what struck him most was the quiet. Swallows swooped through the sky and called to each other, but otherwise that was it. The air was still and warm, undisturbed by the hum of traffic and human interference.

With the march out to their destination over, Liam and the rest of the platoon had then split off into their sections to dig scrapes and bed in for the night, all under the guise of setting up subsurface observation posts.

'You've got to love the army's approach to team-building,' said Biggs. 'Send us halfway round the world to a country full of dangerous animals, and have us digging holes. Fucking genius.'

'Good day for a barbecue,' said Cordner, stretching his back and staring up at the sky, which was swimming-pool blue. 'Not that I'd eat any of it if Pearce was cooking.'

'You saying I can't cook?' Pearce replied.

'I'm saying you could burn water. A chef you ain't.'

Liam immediately discovered that digging out in the Kenyan heat was nothing like doing it back in the UK. Here, rain didn't come to cool you off and the breeze was non-existent. And if the work wasn't shared and managed well, people were liable to get pissed off very quickly and take it out on each other.

'Some beach volleyball wouldn't go amiss,' said Fish, one of the other lads from his section who Liam had recently met. His real name was Kamil Jackson, but he'd been given the nickname 'Fish' because he hated seafood.

'Suck it up,' said Adam Bale, another of the lads in his section. All Liam knew about him was that he'd spent a few of his teenage years stealing cars.

'Pearce complains about everything,' said Cordner. 'It's part of his charm.'

'You're not saying you enjoy it?' asked Pearce, glancing over at Bale. The two were a similar size, but Bale, though fit, lacked the steel-wire muscle of Pearce. Liam knew who he would put his money on if the heat got to them both and they decided to have a go.

Neil Airey then joined in. Unlike the rest, he'd yet to stop digging and was just carrying on with measured deliberate moves, seemingly incapable of experiencing muscle fatigue and exhaustion, even in the relentless heat. The last member of the eight-man section Liam had been placed with, he had the face of a boxer and the knuckles to match.

'It's not about enjoying it,' he said, throwing soil to the side. 'It's about your mind-set. That's all this is. To test you in the heat. See if you can take it.'

'I can take it,' said Pearce. 'So don't go thinking I can't, you got me?'

'All I can see is that you've stopped digging to whine on about it,' said Airey. 'So like Bale said, suck it up, or shut the fuck up.'

Pearce looked to Liam for support. 'You agree this is bollocks, right, RB?'

'RB?' asked Airey. 'Thought your name was Scott.'

'It is,' said Liam. 'But these bastards decided it wasn't good enough.'

Cordner then quickly explained what had happened. 'So Ration Bag seemed like a decent name for him,' he said, concluding the story of Liam's cock-up during the LRCC to roars of laughter from the others. 'RB for short. He won't go making the same mistake again, that's for sure.'

'Well, we'll find out later, won't we?' said Biggs. 'Seeing as this is where we're going to be sleeping for a few nights. Assuming Pearce can pull his thumb out of his arse and get digging again.'

When the scrape was at last dug and camouflaged, Liam was on with the SLR and spotting scope. He'd already checked his kit three times to make sure nothing had gone missing.

'You're a grafter, I'll give you that,' said Waterman, who was in the scrape with Liam, Cordner and Fish.

Shirtless, his tattoos were on full view. Every time he moved, twisted faces from horror movies grimaced at Liam like they were trying to escape from Waterman's body. 'It's like Airey said – it's not about the digging, it's about whether you can just get on with it regardless. Nicely done.'

Liam didn't quite know what to say in reply and just went with, 'Thanks.'

'People think any specialism like Recce Platoon or UKSF or whatever is sexy and cool because it's all danger and derring-do,' said Waterman. 'But it isn't. Most of the time it's dull as shit. It's all about whether you can handle it – the pressure of being close to the enemy, and quiet enough so as not to get slotted.'

'You been in long?' asked Liam.

'Long enough,' said Waterman. 'Eighteen months. I'm up next, so give me a kick in four hours.'

And with that, Liam was alone in the darkening silence. The Kenyan night shrouded the ground in an eerie grey, and soon all he could hear was the sounds of nocturnal animals hunting, hiding, feeding, surviving. And out there too, Liam knew, was Al Shabaab. He wondered just how close.

7

Liam was standing with the rest of the Recce Platoon out in the training area that doubled as a parade ground. It was the start of a new day and a new week. He could hardly believe seven days had gone already. But then they'd been kept busy, with no time left over at the end of each day to do much apart from collapse and grab some rest. The heat didn't help, but he had eventually acclimatized. Fluids were vital to surviving it and he was drinking litres of the stuff – he was determined not to make the same mistake twice and get dehydrated.

The air was thick with the scent of soil and dirt. The heat, Liam had quickly discovered, was different to that he'd experienced in Afghanistan. There it had been a desert heat, dry and ferocious like a blast from an open oven. But here it was more humid, though just as blisteringly hot. The moisture in the air brought with it the rich musk of vegetation. The chill of the previous night had lifted quickly and, along with his breakfast, had done little to refresh Liam's still groggy head. For whatever reason, he had slept too heavily the night before, and was now trying to get his head into gear. Rubbing his eyes yet again in an attempt to push energy into himself and start sparking, Liam stared at what was now sitting in front of them.

Just over an hour ago, close to 200 KDF soldiers had arrived at the camp in a collection of military vehicles that Liam thought wouldn't have looked out of place in a museum. Preceded by a thick cloud that had been more exhaust fumes than dust, the KDF were now sat on the ground waiting for what Liam and the rest of the Recce Platoon were there to provide: world-class training. Liam rubbed his eyes even harder.

'Doesn't fill you with confidence, does it?' It was Cordner, and he was staring at the vehicles the KDF had arrived in.

'I've seen trucks in better nick after they've been slammed by a pissed-off Apache,' said Pearce. 'How the hell they made it here, I don't know.'

From ageing troop carriers to American Humvees, the mismatched collection seemed to Liam almost embarrassed at their state of repair. Leaning at odd angles, with barely a panel unscathed, patches of oil were already beginning to pool underneath them.

'The soldiers look capable, though,' said Liam, looking for something good to say. If he was honest, he'd half expected the soldiers to look like the vehicles, but they were nothing of the sort. They seemed fit, disciplined and keen. Their clothing and kit, though not as up to date as that of Liam and the rest of Recce Platoon, was still fit for purpose and the camouflage pattern was darker. Their webbing was very much like what the British Army had worn a number of years ago, which had now been replaced with the superb modular system issued during Afghanistan.

'Capable they may well be,' said Waterman, 'but did you cop a look at their kit?'

'What about it?' asked Liam.

Although none of the soldiers were armed at that moment, they had all arrived carrying what they'd need for the weeks ahead.

'Did you not clock their weapons?' Waterman asked. 'Christ alive – looked like they'd raided some poor fucker's gun collection!'

Liam thought back and recalled exactly what Waterman was getting at. He knew as well as anyone else that the general approach with most armed forces was standardization. Everyone in Recce Platoon was pretty much armed with SA80s, unless in a specialized role, and given either the Sharpshooter or sniper rifle. The principle was simple: have everyone train with, and use, the same equipment, thus making it easier for them to pick it up wherever they are and carry on with the fight. Supply is made simpler too. From all they'd seen, though, it was clear to Liam that the Kenyan Defence Force had a different approach entirely.

'I reckon half of what these lads carry would either jam or misfire,' said Waterman. 'They've got some decent kit like MP5s and SCARs but it's the other stuff that worries me. It's crazy.'

The MP5, though an old design, was universally famous, not just because it was ferociously reliable and an outstanding weapon for close-quarter fighting, but also because of its association with the SAS. The SCAR, or Special Operations Forces Combat Assault Rifle, was another matter altogether. Recently supplied by the US, and built by FN Herstal, the SCAR was a modular rifle available in both 5.56mm and 7.62 calibres. With the option of different barrel lengths for either close-quarters battle or longer-range operations, it was a superb multi-purpose weapon built to satisfy most if not all combat roles.

'There's even a few AKs in there,' said Pearce. 'And if they're in as shit a state as the ones we've all used in 'Stan, then they couldn't shoot my bollocks off at point blank.'

'That's because you haven't got any bollocks,' said Liam, but his attention was mostly on the captain.

Captain Owusu had already addressed everyone about what the next few weeks would involve, and was now talking to a group of KDF officers. Liam tried to zone in on what was being said but was unable to make anything out.

'I guess this is where we get to meet and greet,' said Pearce. 'I'm looking all right, aren't I? My make-up isn't smudged or anything?'

'It's like a blind date,' said Cordner. 'So just stick to the simple stuff – name, age, interests. No mention of trying to get to second base, though. That's just rude and way too fecking forward.'

'Not sure Pearce has ever been on a date,' said Fish. 'And if he has, she must've been blind.'

At last, Captain Owusu came over to the platoon, casting a long shadow on the ground in front of him.

The bright sun was already burning the exposed skin on Liam's arms, and his clothes stuck to him. The meaty sweet smell of sweat hung in the air. At first it turned the nose, but pretty soon it blended into the surroundings. That didn't make it any less unpleasant, though.

'A few things to be aware of,' said the captain, addressing the soldiers a little distance away from the KDF. 'First, as you've already witnessed, their equipment is a little, shall we say, varied? In the light of recent events involving Al Shabaab, the Kenyan government is working hard to re-equip its entire armed forces. But it can't do it all at once and is somewhat dependent on generous donations from overseas.'

'That would explain the SCARs,' said a soldier at the back of the group.

'Exactly,' said the captain. 'Some of their kit is seriously up to date, some of it not so much. And the same goes for their training. The KDF is racing not just to keep up with the rest of the world, but to handle the threat it now faces. It even has a small unit of special forces soldiers trained to deal with terrorists.'

'If that's the case, then why are we here?' asked Biggs.

'By small, I mean tiny,' explained Captain Owusu. 'Fifty soldiers at this current time, their numbers building slowly but surely. So, not really enough to deal with what they are facing. And those soldiers are otherwise engaged, so using them in a training capacity would be a huge waste of valuable – and at this current time, rare – resources.'

It made sense, thought Liam. There was no point spending a stack of cash on a small number of troops and then using them as teachers. It made much more sense, politically as well as financially, to bring in the

British. Which is where he and the rest of the Recce Platoon came in.

'Despite how they look, this is no ragtag army,' continued the captain. 'They are good soldiers in the main. Fit and capable and no slouch in a fight. It is also worth bearing in mind that many of the lads in front of you have had first-hand experience of dealing with Al Shabaab. They've seen combat, some of it as fierce and brutal as anything we ourselves have dealt with. So my advice to all of you right here and now is to accept that, although you may be here to teach them, you will probably learn a thing or two from them too. So be prepared to listen.'

This was something else that reminded Liam of his time in Afghanistan. He had been lucky enough to work closely with the Afghan National Army – the ANA – and one soldier in particular, Zaman Shah, had become a good friend. He'd not only helped him with his Dari, the local language where Liam had been deployed, but had saved his life.

'One final thing,' said Captain Owusu, and his voice lowered as if speaking conspiratorially. 'A lot of these soldiers can seem a little bit, how shall we say, wired? The reason for this is because in Kenya, *khat* is legal. And for those of you who've never heard of it, all you need to know is that it's a plant with stimulant properties.

Imagine sipping on Red Bull and smoking cigarettes all day and you'll have some idea of its effect. And if they're not chewing it now, they definitely will be when they go up against Al Shabaab. You'll probably be offered some too. All UK troops are banned from taking khat.'

The captain then turned to walk over to the Kenyan officers and soon the KDF soldiers were on their feet.

'You ready for this?' asked Waterman, who was at Liam's side, looking at the lines of soldiers now staring back at them.

'Not sure what I'm supposed to be ready for,' replied Liam. 'I worked with the ANA a fair bit. How different can it be?'

Waterman had no chance to answer as Biggs called the section together, splitting them away from the rest of the platoon.

'Captain Owusu has advised us to work this in twos,' he said. 'That way we won't be tripping over each other.'

'Remind me again what we're doing?' asked Pearce.

'Were you listening during the briefing earlier?'

'Yes' – Pearce nodded – 'but I don't think Bale was. Lots of big words were used and he struggles beyond two syllables.'

'I'm not sure what's more surprising,' said Biggs. 'That you were listening, or that you just used the word syllables.'

'Fuck off,' said Pearce.

'Right.' Biggs ignored Pearce's grumbling. 'For the benefit of everyone other than Mr Student of the Year over here, the next few days will involve us training these guys in CTR. Each pair will be given a small platoon to work with. Clear?'

Liam nodded, though deep down he was concerned. He was no trainer or instructor. So how the hell was he supposed to teach Close Target Reconnaissance to a bunch of Kenyan soldiers – some of them much older and apparently more experienced in combat than he himself was. He had to instruct them in how to sneak up on the enemy with minimal kit and collect intelligence, but this wasn't like learning long division at school – there could be serious and potentially life-threatening consequences if the Kenyans were deployed without the skills they needed. And it was down to him – an experienced soldier, sure, but still only a nineteen-year-old – to make sure they acquired those skills and could put them into practice.

Fifteen minutes later and Liam, alongside Waterman, was standing in front of an expectant group of KDF soldiers.

'So, you want to flip a coin to see who starts this off?' asked Waterman.

Liam was about to say yes when he changed his mind.

ANDY McNAB

'No, I'll get this going. May as well just jump in at the deep end, right?'

Waterman nodded, a faint grin etched on his face, then stepped back to allow Liam to take the floor.

Liam moved forward. To have so many eyes on him was unnerving. And though Waterman was all but a pace behind him, he felt very exposed. These soldiers were looking to him for leadership, guidance. Well, he thought, time to show that these fresh lance corporal pips weren't given for nothing . . .

'Scott?'

Liam glanced over to Waterman. 'What's up?'

They were both hunched up behind some bushes and observing, to their left and right, two four-man teams carrying out a CTR on makeshift positions held by the other two four-man teams. Darkness had descended and they were both using the head-mounted monocular night vision, a piece of kit now issued to all infantry soldiers and clipped to the front of their helmets.

'Nothing's up,' replied Waterman. 'And that's my point. These guys are properly switched on. I'm impressed.'

Waterman had a point, thought Liam. Having instructed the soldiers on the finer arts of camouflage and concealment, he and Waterman had then outlined the role of each member of a four-man CTR team. With

80

one as point man tasked to collect intelligence, one as a relay point between the point man and the rest of the company, and the two others in fire support in case things kicked off, they had then split their group into four teams of four. The aim was to give each one the opportunity to work together on a CTR, with two acting as the enemy while the other two carried out the recce without – hopefully – getting pinged.

Now, as they were heading into night time, the KDF soldiers were on to the practical side of things. And it was going very well. A part of Liam hoped it was in some ways down to his and Waterman's knowledge and teaching, but he knew that the main praise lay with the soldiers. And one in particular had caught his attention.

'They're good,' he said, 'but Odull is doing this like he was made for it.'

Of the sixteen soldiers they had been allocated, Jacob Odull had stood out immediately. He was a tower of a man – Liam guessed he was around six foot six, built like a tank – and he had a laugh that rolled out of him like a bowling ball trundling its way to the pins at the end of the lane. Even though he could have only been in his early twenties, the other soldiers clearly held him in high esteem, looking to him as their natural leader.

'You heard that one of his brothers was killed by Al Shabaab?' asked Waterman.

'Yeah,' Liam answered. 'He wants to join that special forces unit Owusu was on about.'

'I bet he does,' said Waterman. 'Payback is a hell of a motivator.'

With the exercise drawing to a close, Liam and Waterman pulled the soldiers together to recap and then sent them off for some much-needed kip.

As they were leaving, a voice called out. 'Lance Corporal Scott?'

Liam turned to find himself looking up at Odull. God, the guy was massive . . . 'Odull?'

'I would like to thank you for this training.'

Liam didn't know what to say. He was, after all, just doing his job. 'I hope it will come in useful,' he said eventually.

'It will,' said Odull. 'It will help us.'

'Al Shabaab sound pretty serious,' said Liam, then wished he'd kept his mouth shut. *Pretty serious* did no justice at all to what Odull had suffered with the loss of his brother. Liam himself had lost friends in battle, but to lose a family member was on another level completely.

'Yes,' said Odull. 'They killed one of my brothers. I would like to return the favour many times over.'

Liam noticed a fierceness in the big man's eyes. It was unnerving.

Odull spoke again. 'My other brother, they kidnapped him also. I have no idea if he is alive or dead. Perhaps soon I will find out.'

Liam remembered what Captain Owusu had told them about the recent attack on BATUK. 'He was taken from here?'

Odull nodded. 'I am the eldest. It is my responsibility to get him back. My mother, all she does now is cry and pray for his return.'

'Has there been any word from Al Shabaab?' asked Liam.

'Only ransoms and demands,' said Odull. 'We know only that the hostages, if they are still alive, are somewhere in Somalia.'

'I truly hope that they are,' said Liam.

Odull said nothing more and strolled off into the dark.

'What was all that about?' asked Waterman. 'You looked very solemn.'

'He has another brother,' said Liam. 'He was one of the soldiers kidnapped three weeks ago.'

'Holy fucking shit,' said Waterman.

'I don't think that even comes close,' Liam replied.

The training had carried on as planned, but on the fourth evening the KDF soldiers had suddenly been summoned. They'd grabbed their kit and left the camp in as much of a rush as they could achieve in their worn-out vehicles. It had got everyone talking, and Captain Owusu had called Recce Platoon to an unscheduled briefing. Now the whole of Recce Platoon was sitting together in one of the canvas shelters used at BATUK for briefing purposes. Even though the sun was setting, heat still seemed to radiate from the ground and the air was dead.

Captain Owusu was in front of the platoon. Behind him was a screen, and in front, a laptop attached to a projector.

'Right, everyone, I'll come straight to the point: what was originally a training posting is now for real. We have been informed by the KDF that a key Al Shabaab figure has been sighted close to the border. And what makes this even more interesting is that he is a British national.'

If the platoon was quiet before, it was deathly silent now. Liam leaned forward, not wanting to miss anything the captain was about to tell them.

'What I am about to show you is the terrorist in question's rise to fame. Some of it is graphic.'

Owusu bent down, fiddled with the laptop, and a few seconds later a movie started to play out behind him. He stepped back to allow everyone a good view of what was happening.

'The man in question is Abdul Azeez,' he went on. Liam watched as the footage showed a bearded man wearing a white shalwar kameez – a long baggy tunic and loose trousers – climb into the passenger seat of a Toyota pick-up. Armed with an AK47, the club badge of any self-respecting Al Qaeda terrorist, he smiled at the camera as though he was heading off on a family outing.

'A British citizen,' continued the captain, 'his real name is actually Andrew Bradford. Brought up in Birmingham, he converted to Islam in his teens and changed his name.'

The scene shifted, and now the film showed Azeez standing with a group of other similarly dressed men who were all cheering and waving their own AKs in the air.

'At the age of eighteen, he went to university and completed a degree in chemical engineering. On graduation, he purchased a round-the-world ticket and, so his parents believed, went off travelling.'

Again the movie changed, this time showing a group of men on their knees, all blindfolded, arms tied behind their backs. Walking up and down in front of them was Azeez. When he wasn't smiling at the camera, he was poking the men with the barrel of his weapon.

'Turns out that his "travelling" was little more than a clever way to get out of the country and into the thick of Al Shabaab's activities in Somalia.'

When the captain's voice fell silent, Liam watched as Azeez, a beaming smile still stapled to his face, turned his weapon on the kneeling men and opened fire.

'We know that he rose quickly through the ranks, buoyed along by his charm and charisma, but also his brutality.'

With the murdered men now all on the ground, fresh bullet wounds bleeding their clothes red, Azeez then casually slipped a fresh magazine into his weapon and walked over to make doubly sure none of them would be getting up ever again.

'He may still only be in his late twenties,' said the captain, 'but Azeez is a major player. He's worked as a military commander and recruiter, and is rapidly becoming Al Shabaab's poster boy.'

The screen went blank. No one spoke. Liam had no doubt that, like him, everyone was reeling from this sudden change to their role. What they'd just seen on the screen had brought home the reality of it with all the subtlety of a pissed-off rhino.

'The INT we have received suggests that Azeez is in the area because an attack is imminent. And if he is running it, then there's a good chance it isn't just a few well-placed IEDs either. He will be after a headline grabber, something that'll up Al Shabaab's profile – and his own. Any questions?'

Liam raised his hand. 'Where's the INT come from? How do we know it's reliable?' Back in Afghanistan, he'd been on the wrong end of unreliable intelligence after heading out to find a weapons cache that didn't exist – and a sniper who definitely *did*.

'A number of undercover operators have provided this intelligence. Of those operating inside Al Shabaab, two of them were killed in the video you just saw.'

Liam had never really given much thought to the murkier world of counter terrorism. His job had always involved going up against a known enemy, armed and ready. But now he was faced with the reality that others were right in the thick of it, risking their lives every day to stop attacks from the inside. And they were getting killed in the process.

'Our new role is this,' said Captain Owusu. 'The Kenyan forces have brought forward a planned deployment into Somalia. It will be our job to lead them in.'

8

'Lieutenant Young has really missed his true calling,' said Biggs.

The sergeant was sitting with Liam and the rest of Recce Platoon around an astonishingly detailed model of the area they were soon to be sent into. After last night's revelation, the platoon had all got up early, scoffed breakfast, and been called together for Captain Owusu to relay his orders.

'That's art, that is, right there,' agreed Cordner. 'Should be in the Tate.'

Liam looked down at the model. He had to agree with Biggs – it really was the work of an artist. Measuring a good ten metres by five metres, and surrounded by sandbags to prevent anyone from accidentally walking over it and destroying it, the model was one of the best he had ever seen. Liam was used to seeing something a little more slipshod, with a few rocks here and there to indicate obstacles, sticks as roads or trails, and the occasional battered, rusting tin to indicate some kind of building. Once, he'd even seen someone's worn-out sock used to represent the checkpoint they had, at the time, been occupying. When asked why, the soldier in question had replied, 'Because this place stinks and is full of holes.'

But this model was on another level altogether. Liam could make out mountains and valleys, even a river, all crafted from the soil and dirt that lay around them. Liam's own skills in model building were embarrassingly bad. But he wasn't alone. Soldiers, in the main, didn't seem to be artistic by nature, at least as far as he'd experienced during his time in the infantry. And anyone who could produce something this good was more valuable than gold, or, in soldier terms, than a fresh, unread copy of a top-shelf glossy magazine.

Captain Owusu stood up in front of them, and everyone immediately fell silent. 'Before we start,' he said, 'I think we all owe the clearly talented Lieutenant Young a round of applause for this rather excellent rendering of the zone we'll be operating in. Frankly, I've never seen anything like it. Well done, Lieutenant!'

Liam and the rest of the lads clapped and cheered. The atmosphere was relaxed, but that didn't mean none of them was taking it seriously. Quite the opposite, observed Liam, checking out the faces of those sitting and standing with him around the model. Everyone was studying it intently, already recording it in their memory, imagining being there on the ground. Maps were good, but seeing the geography of an area like this gave everyone a visual hook to hold onto. And that often made a big difference when they went in for real.

'You are all far too kind,' said Lieutenant Young. 'I do portraits as well, by the way. Fifty quid a pop, if anyone wants something to send home to their lovely ladies. I'll even try and make you good-looking.'

'Even Pearce?' chimed Fish.

'Well, I did say *try*,' replied the lieutenant.

Captain Owusu waited for the laughter to subside, then got on with running through the task that now faced them.

'In simple terms, gentlemen, the KDF are taking the fight to the enemy. With Abdul Azeez having been sighted, they want to strike hard and fast. But to do so, they hope, with minimal risk to life – either theirs or any civilians in the area. Clearly this is a tall order in a combative situation, but even more so considering what they will be facing. Which is where we play our part, and you get to prove that all the money spent on your specialized training was actually a good investment.'

Minimal risk to life? thought Liam. That was

understandable, but judging by the terrain they were going into, and the ruthlessness of the enemy they were up against, that was indeed a tall order. Bullets fly, people die; it was the hard reality of what happened in a battle, be that close quarter or on a larger scale. He knew that as well as anyone here. They'd all been in firefights and experienced the snap and crack of rifle fire coming in heavy.

Lieutenant Young took the stage. 'It's our understanding that we'll be operating between ten and fifteen kilometres in front of the KDF,' he said, pointing at the map with a thin length of bamboo cane. 'We will make our way into the Kismayo district of the Lower Juba region of Somalia. Though not under direct Al Shabaab control, the terrorists have established themselves here as it is close to the Kenyan border. And it's from here that they've been launching their attacks and increasing their influence in the region.

'We will cross this river' – he pointed at the model – 'then move into these hills, here. Working in your sections, the aim is to get eyes on where most of the terrorist movement has been observed. Anything and everything you see will be relayed back to the KDF. When we believe there is sufficient INT to go on to guide them to their objectives, Recce Platoon will lead them in, and the KDF will advance on the positions we have identified.'

ANDY McNAB

'So we won't be required to fight?'

The question came from a soldier sitting opposite Liam. It was Corporal Slater, a lad Liam knew mainly because he was difficult to miss. The nickname 'Bull' suited him well – his hobby was weight-training and he was massive. It wasn't asked in a gung-ho way, as though he was itching to get into the thick of it and let off the safety on his SA80. Instead, it was a simple, matter-of-fact query. These were men who wanted the facts straight. They were trained to fight and weren't afraid to do so if it was necessary.

'We are here in a supporting role,' said Captain Owusu. 'Politically, this is very sensitive. The Kenyans need to be seen to be taking the lead on this and our task is to keep as low a profile as possible. They want Al Shabaab to know they are unwelcome, in the most forceful way possible.'

Another soldier raised his arm. This time it was Lance Corporal Parker, a quiet guy who generally spent his free time reading or doing long distance running. He also wrote poetry. No one took the piss – his stuff was actually excellent. 'Do we have the right to engage if things get sticky?'

'The aim is to ensure that they don't,' said Lieutenant Young. 'This is, after all, subsurface and Close Target Recce. And that means making sure you're not spotted.'

'But what if we are?' Parker continued. 'If we get pinged, I'm assuming we don't just stand up, wave a hello, and apologize for playing I-spy?'

A rumble of laughter made its way around the model.

'You will work this to the letter,' said Captain Owusu. 'No unnecessary risks are to be taken. Getting caught by Al Shabaab is something nobody wants. You all saw how Azeez deals with prisoners. His reputation is built on his ruthlessness and it's safe to say he thoroughly enjoys killing the enemy, particularly first hand and up close. So, if things do turn bad, and the proverbial poop hits the air-con, you get out fast, using whatever force is necessary to get clear. I'm sure I don't need to waste my time telling you why. We do not wish to see a repeat of what happened in Mogadishu.'

Owusu stood back, and once again Lieutenant Young spoke to the platoon. He may have been a fair few years younger than the captain, but he spoke with assured confidence and authority.

'At midday we will be taken by Chinook to a forward operating base close to the border with Somalia. The FOB lies inside the Boni National Reserve, which runs along the border and down to the Indian Ocean. The FOB itself is little more than a clearing and at less than twenty-four hours old, Al Shabaab will have no idea that it even exists.'

This made total sense, thought Liam, and would explain the sudden departure of the KDF the night before. They must have been sent ahead to make the area ready for the operation. There was no point planning an offensive and trying to keep it secret if they were then going to do it from an FOB that Al Shabaab probably already had eyes on. They'd be spooked if they noticed major troop movements.

'And that,' concluded Lieutenant Young, 'is all you need to know for now. So I suggest we all spend the next few hours getting our kit up to scratch. Dismissed.'

'All sorted?' Biggs was standing at the end of Liam's cot, kitted up and ready to go.

Liam responded with a nod. After Captain Owusu's briefing, the platoon had gone into overdrive. Weapons were stripped, checked and double-checked. Kit was collected. And in a few minutes, they would be off.

Like everyone else in the platoon, Liam was armed with his SA80 and carrying 300 rounds. The SA80 bayonet was clipped to his belt. In addition to this, he was carrying the recently issued Glock 17 Gen 4 pistol. Lighter than the Browning pistol, which had been the mainstay of the army for years, it was also considerably more accurate. And with an increased magazine capacity of seventeen 9mm rounds it gave the individual soldier four additional chances to stop a threat to his own life and those around him. His bergen was packed with his usual equipment, including doss bag, clothing and a waterproof Gore-tex jacket, and half of his forty-eight hours' worth of rations. The other half he carried in his webbing, with his medical kit and other necessities. They may have all received medical and survival training, but that training only came into play if the worst came to the worst. Liam had no urge to put those skills to the test.

Satisfied that everything was in order, he fell in behind Waterman and joined the rest of his section outside their sleeping quarters. From there it was a quick walk to where two Chinooks were waiting to take them to their next location.

'Nice of the army to take us on a sightseeing trip, eh?' said Cordner as they made their way towards the helicopters.

'Reckon we'll be able to send postcards?' Liam asked.

Closing in on the Chinooks, conversation ceased, the thrum of the twin rotor blades and the roar of the engines drowning out all other sound. Climbing in, Liam strapped himself into his seat and closed his eyes. A lot had changed in the last twenty-four hours, he thought. As for what the next twenty-four held, he could only wonder.

* * *

Just under three hours later, in mid-afternoon, the platoon landed at the FOB. It was action stations as soon as their boots hit the dirt, as the platoon split into sections and got down to business. Around them, the KDF were busy erecting shelters and distributing kit.

A map was on the ground and Biggs was crouched down beside it. 'Pretty shortly, we will be driven across the border with Somalia here,' he said, pointing to it. 'We will then, under cover of darkness, make our way here.' Biggs's finger rested on a ridge overlooking a slim valley running east to west. 'Here we split into two four-man teams and set up two subsurface positions. Our targets are here, and here.' He pointed. Drawn on the map in red were two simple crosses. The sergeant moved his finger back a fraction to a blue circle. 'This is where we will set up a dead-letter drop. The KDF will then keep this stocked with equipment and we will relay back and forth with our INT, returning with supplies.'

'So what exactly are we copping a look at?' asked Fish. 'We talking a couple of shacks in the jungle, or a full-on holiday camp for trainee terrorists?'

'That remains quite literally to be seen,' said Biggs. 'Anything that Al Shabaab has established in this kind of terrain will be well-camouflaged and pretty damned temporary. The INT suggests that they've a number of dens along this valley, but as to size and number no one's got a clue. So with us and the rest of the lads having a sneaky look-see, we're hoping we can catch them at whatever it is they're up to.'

'We've only got forty-eight hours' worth of food and water,' Liam pointed out. 'There's no way it's going to last us if we're pegged out there for God knows how long.'

'Which is why,' replied Biggs, 'we will be fully dependent on a supply chain provided by the KDF. They know the area well. Dead-letter drops will be established and we will use them to swap all our INT – maps, memory cards, whatever we find – with water, food and anything else we need.

'We'll work in the teams we're used to. So that's me, Pearce, Cordner and Scott. And Waterman, Jackson, Bale and Airey. We'll be in touch with each other on our PRRs.'

Liam was pleased to hear that they would all have Personal Role Radios. The small transmitter-receiver radios had made a huge difference to soldiers on patrol, and communication was now immediate rather than whispered up and down the line or sent by a complex code of hand signals.

'Then what?' asked Waterman. 'I'm assuming we're not just sitting in a hole for a couple of weeks, then winging it back here for a pat on the back and a brew.'

'Not exactly, no,' said a voice from behind them. It was Lieutenant Young. 'If we need to, we'll be sending some of you back in on CTR. The KDF don't want to miss anything. And if there's a chance to sneak in and grab Abdul Azeez, even better.'

'So it's a possible smash and grab?' asked Pearce. 'Bags me in on that.'

'For now,' said the lieutenant, 'focus on getting in, collecting as much INT as you can, and getting out safely. And in case you're interested, your limousine awaits . . .' He nodded across the clearing to a knackered old pick-up with a canvas hood.

'Not what I'm used to,' said Cordner. 'I'm more of a Rolls-Royce kind of guy.'

The truck, observed Liam, looked like it had spent its life on a farm and had been sent to them for one last job before being allowed to die.

'There's less chance of you being noticed in that than if you drive into Somalia in a Humvee,' said Lieutenant Young. 'And I'm sure you'll all appreciate the aroma of manure in the back. Now get shifting – you've work to do.'

The lieutenant turned and marched off. Without another word spoken, Liam and the rest of the section were on their feet and jogging over to the truck. The driver got out to welcome them.

'Odull!' said Liam.

The big man grinned back. 'I will be driving you today, Lance Corporal Scott.'

'Fuck me, that dude really is massive,' whispered Pearce. 'How did he even fit in the driver's seat?'

Odull moved to the back of the pick-up, unhooked the tailgate, then flipped the canvas hood up.

'I am sorry it is not more luxurious,' he said. 'But I have swept it out. The smell I could do nothing about.'

Liam clambered in, with the others following behind. 'Cosy,' he said as he dropped himself onto the flatbed, and he was soon squashed up tight against the driver's cabin.

'It's a safety feature,' said Cordner. 'No seatbelts, so pack us in so tight that we can't actually move if there's a crash. Pure fecking genius.'

Odull heaved the tailgate back into place. 'I will drive as carefully as I can,' he said. 'But the track is not good.'

'How long is the journey?' Fish asked.

'It will take us about two hours,' Odull replied. 'If you need anything, just knock on the cabin. If I see something ahead, I will do the same.'

'By something ahead, you mean Al Shabaab?' asked Airey.

'It is hard to say,' Odull replied. 'Al Shabaab have been in Somalia for a long time. They have recruited even children to their cause.' He pulled down the hood. Then the engine grumbled into life and they were on their way.

'Children?' said Liam.

'Life for them is hard,' explained Biggs. 'Most of them are starving as it is. All it takes is the promise of some fruit and a pair of shoes, and you've got an eleven-year-old kid running around with an AK47 in his hands.'

'You mean there's a chance we could end up being shot at by kids?' Liam asked. 'And having to return fire?' He'd never even considered that as a possibility. Adults, yes, because they at least had some say in what they had decided to do. But children?

'Best not to think about it,' said Biggs. 'If we do this well, then we hopefully won't actually get shot at by anyone.'

From then on, no one spoke. Instead, they made use of the time to get some shut-eye. Uncomfortable it may have been, but if there was one thing all soldiers knew how to do, it was how to sleep anywhere.

They woke up in darkness as the truck pulled to a halt. On the equator, the sun set quickly and early, and now the stars were out. The trip, though uncomfortable, had thankfully gone without hitch or pause. After being dropped off by Odull, Liam and the rest of the section made their way on towards their destination.

Once far enough away from the track not to be spotted from anyone driving by, they had quickly got their bearings and then set off. Their navigation skills were immediately put to the test, and along with their maps and compasses, they took frequent glances at the sky in order to use the stars as markers. Regular checks every couple of hundred metres ensured that they never wandered too far from the quickest route to their destination. They passed the dead-letter drop – a well-hidden cleft in a small crag concealed by brush and small acacia trees. Empty now, in the next twenty-four hours it would be filled with fresh supplies.

In Afghanistan, the terrain had been rocks and mountains and thick scrub that tore at your boots. Here, it was greener, the countryside more rolling. Then there was the wildlife. At first, it had taken Liam's eyes a while to adjust to what he was seeing, but soon he felt like he was walking through a BBC David Attenborough pro-gramme. He could hear the howls and snarls of wild dogs, and in the distance he spied the distinctive silhouettes of a herd of giraffes. Odull had told him that lions sometimes roamed the area, although Liam was very relieved not to encounter any. Mosquitoes swarmed around their faces and flies emerged from the long grass underfoot, disturbed by their movement. Despite being bitten God knows how many times, Liam still felt very lucky. The wilderness was as beautiful as it was dangerous, and being there was an experience he found difficult to describe.

Approximately six hours later, the section arrived where Biggs had shown them on the map – a ridge, slipping down on the other side into a thin valley below. It was still dark, but dawn was approaching and there was no time to dig in properly.

'This is where we split up,' said Biggs, turning to Waterman's team. 'You know what to do: get yourselves undercover sharpish and stay out of sight during daylight. As soon as night falls, get dug in and hidden. And stay in touch. Call in on the PRR every two hours even if nothing is happening. We all need to be aware of what's going on. Understood?'

There were silent nods all round.

'We've got two hours max,' the sergeant continued. 'We need to be out of sight and quiet before the sun decides to shine a halo on our location. So no fucking around. We're in the badlands now. Any questions?'

The only question Liam had was just what they had let themselves in for.

9

'RB?'

Liam was on with the SLR. The SD card was close to full and he had thirty minutes left taking photographs of anything that looked out of place or betrayed possible human activity. He kept his eye at the camera, and answered, 'Yes, boss?'

'It's your turn to go for replen, mate,' said Biggs. 'We're closing in on the end of our second forty-eight-hour stint. And I'm sure, like me, you're desperate to get your hands on more burgers and beans.'

Having kept out of sight for their first day over-looking the shallow valley, Liam, Biggs, Pearce and Cordner had gone to work digging their hole. The soil had been soft, but the roots of the surrounding plants were gnarly and thick. Their entrenching tools had served them well, cutting and hacking through, but at points they'd had to improvise, falling back on the saw blades in the pocket survival kits they all carried at their own personal expense.

Once dug, they'd covered the scrape with netting, keeping it from sagging too much into the hole with stakes stuck into the ground. With leaves and twigs threaded through, the whole thing had then been thoroughly covered with anything to hand and it was almost dangerously invisible. Liam had, once or twice on leaving it, been at a loss as to how to find it again, which was both unnerving and comforting. If he couldn't see it, having helped to create the thing, then anyone who didn't know it was there in the first place wouldn't have a chance.

Biggs and Liam were the only ones awake, with Cordner and Pearce taking their shift at grabbing some shuteye. The hole had certainly grown ripe, the reek of four unwashed men and all their kit leaving nothing to the imagination.

'You mean Cordner didn't put in the order for steak and beer we requested?'

'Wouldn't matter even if he had,' said Biggs. 'You've seen his writing. Looks like a snail trail. Anything new to report back?'

Liam shook his head. 'Nothing more than what we've

already seen. Those two sites we were supposed to observe are still empty. But there's definitely movement on that trail Pearce spotted.'

'He has some uses, it seems,' said Biggs. 'And that movement corresponds with what Waterman's lot have seen from their post.'

'I still don't get how the KDF didn't know there was a camp down there,' said Liam.

'The satellite photographs we were given were taken a week ago,' said Biggs. 'These kind of camps are built and occupied as quickly as they are abandoned. How's your map coming along?'

'Piss off,' said Liam. 'I don't see why it's down to me to sketch it out.'

'It's a process of elimination, RB,' said Biggs. 'And God knows you need the practice. Have you checked your kit?'

'For what?' Liam asked.

'Well, I've heard stuff can take a wander,' said Biggs. 'You know, just disappear and then suddenly reappear in front of the enemy. Ration bags, for example.'

'Well, aren't you the comedian?' said Liam.

'And I'm here all night,' said Biggs.

Liam shook his head, knowing he'd never live down the incident from the LRCC. He looked back at his map. Along with the memory cards and any observation notes, hand-drawn maps were also sent back to the dead-letter drop.

Liam snapped another photograph, then turned to stare past Biggs, who was on with the spotting scope.

'So who's going to wake Pearce?'

'I'll leave that pleasure to you as well,' said Biggs. 'No, don't thank me. Honestly, it's fine.'

Considering their situation – they were essentially behind enemy lines and miles away from any serious backup – Liam was actually enjoying himself. They had settled into a well-ordered routine, and as yet no one had fallen out or made any errors. It was also good to know they weren't just training any more, or training someone else, but doing an important job that they all hoped would make a difference.

'I'll give him another fifteen minutes then,' said Liam, putting off the inevitable.

'Scared?'

'Of Pearce, no,' said Liam. 'But of the stink that comes out of his doss bag? Too fucking right I am. Reeks like something crawled up his arse to die.'

Biggs started to laugh, but stopped midway, his expression snapping immediately to serious.

'What is it?' hissed Liam, instinctively dropping his voice, the look on Biggs's face warning enough.

Biggs held up a hand, then pointed at his right ear.

Liam listened in. Focusing, he zoned out the sound of his breathing, his heartbeat, and concentrated on what was happening around them.

Silence.

Liam mouthed, 'What was it?' half wondering if the sergeant was taking the piss – no, more likely testing his reactions. Keeping him on his toes.

Still nothing from Biggs. Then, just as Liam was about to voice his suspicions, he heard it too. The rustle of movement. It was off to their left, down in the valley. Though 'valley', Liam thought, was a very grand description for what was essentially a shallow basin about two kilometres across. The bottom was probably no more than a hundred metres or so below them.

Liam listened for a while longer. Whatever it was, it definitely sounded like it was approaching. Probably more wildlife, he thought. They'd heard plenty of un-explained sounds since arriving, as well as a fair few they all recognized. The cackling howl of a pack of hyenas in particular had sent a chill through Liam and he hoped that the sound wasn't them closing in.

Then he heard something else, and Biggs signed again, this time opening and closing his hand like a mouth. Christ, thought Liam; there were people out there, and they were getting closer. In that moment, he became super aware of everything around him, his senses upping their game. He couldn't just hear the wind playing in the trees, but also bushes twisting and swaying, the faint crack and snap of twigs.

Pearce snored.

Biggs reacted immediately, clamping his hand down on Pearce's face. Pearce was awake in a beat, struggling against the hand over his mouth, but a split second later he realized something was up and lay still. Silent communication between him and Biggs was enough to let him know things could soon turn bad. He rolled over and woke Cordner.

Liam was still listening in. The voices were definitely drawing closer. A nod from Biggs and Liam was back on the SLR to see if he could get eyes on. The zoom lens was excellent, so if there was anything out there he'd be able to see it in high definition. He'd also be able to snap a few photographs off, and that was an added bonus if whoever was approaching them was Al Shabaab.

A couple of minutes later, Pearce and Cordner were out of their bags, SA80s in the shoulder. No one wanted this to kick off, but if it did, they were ready for it.

And still the voices grew closer.

Biggs risked a whisper. 'RB – anything yet?'

Liam shook his head and murmured, 'Pearce – punch through to Waterman. Warn them. And see if they can get a visual.'

As Pearce contacted the other team, Liam kept working with the SLR and Biggs joined in with the spotting scope. Patience paid off.

'Got them,' said Liam. 'Four men approaching. Left. One hundred metres.'

Biggs confirmed it. 'All armed too,' he added softly. 'Fuck . . .'

It was exactly what none of them wanted. Now it was a waiting game, and Liam knew they had no choice but to sit it out. They were there to observe, not go in hot. Even if that meant having someone pretty much walk right over them.

'Fifty metres,' said Liam, and snapped a flurry of photographs. At this range, he had as good a view of them as he could ever want. They were all men, wearing grubby T-shirts and trousers, sandals on their feet. The weapons were AK47s, and at that moment he didn't care if they were in good enough nick to put a hole through a five-pence piece at three hundred metres, or so beaten up they'd miss a Humvee at point blank. That the men were armed was enough. It was as good a sign as any that they weren't just out for an evening stroll.

As the men continued to approach, Liam knew they were all thinking the same thing: had they been pinged? If they had, then surely there would be more than four, for starters. Not only that – wouldn't they have come in hard rather than just doing a walk-by?

The voices were clear now. Liam didn't understand what they were saying, but the tone was telling. They were laughing and chatting, rather than talking in hushed tones. Perhaps they were safe . . . but they couldn't take any chances.

Biggs signed to Liam to make ready with his own SA80. This he did, quickly removing the SD card from the camera. If they were going to have to hightail it out of there, he didn't want to leave behind any of the INT.

Biggs signed again, this time ensuring everyone knew the order of play if it kicked off. Pearce and Cordner would be up and out first, with Biggs and Liam covering them.

Snap.

The sound of a twig breaking just outside their hole made them all freeze. The terrorists must be just a few paces away now, thought Liam. His heart was thumping hard and adrenaline was surging through his veins, readying him for a fight.

A telltale smell slipped through the camouflaged roof. Cigarette smoke, realized Liam – but there was a sweeter note to it as well: cannabis.

He couldn't believe it. Had these four really walked off for a fly smoke to get high?

The next few minutes dragged on and Liam almost wished things would kick off just to break the tension. Then, at last, they heard movement again, this time heading away from them.

Liam waited for a minute or two, then was up again on the SLR. Confirmed: they were moving off. He turned to Biggs and a simple nod was enough. He saw the sergeant relax, but not one of them made a sound for another fifteen minutes.

'Fuck,' said Biggs, at last.

'I'll second that,' said Cordner. 'The smell of that tobacco is like nectar to a bee for me.'

Liam nodded, working on calming himself down from what, a few minutes ago, had seemed very much like it was going to turn into a firefight.

'Can't believe you woke me up for a couple of weedheads,' said Pearce.

Liam had another look through the SLR. 'They've definitely gone. That was close.'

'Look on the bright side,' said Cordner. 'It's as good a confirmation as any that we can play a decent game of hide-and-seek.'

The tension broken, everyone relaxed a little.

'Now that you're awake, Pearce,' said Biggs, 'you're on with RB for replen. It'll be dark in thirty, so make sure you're ready to move that lazy arse of yours.'

'Needs his hand holding, does he?' said Pearce.

'I know where your hands spend most of their time,' said Liam, 'so if it's all the same with you, keep them to yourself.'

'My hands are clean,' replied Pearce.

'Yeah, but your mind isn't,' said Cordner. 'You know you can go blind, don't you?'

Liam looked to Biggs. 'The SD card's full and my map, if you can call it that, is done. Notes?'

The sergeant pulled a pad from a pocket of his jacket and handed it over. 'I'm hoping this is making sense to them back at the FOB,' he said. 'I can't see that having us stay out here much longer is going to be any use.'

Half an hour later, when it was time for Liam and Pearce to head off to the dead-letter drop, Liam clambered across the hole to the only exit.

'Any last-minute requests?'

'A hot-water bottle would be nice,' said Biggs.

'And some proper chocolate, instead of that shite the army puts in the ration packs,' said Cordner.

'Air freshener too,' added Biggs. 'I know we're sent out here for our health, lots of good clean air, but Pearce's arse has ruined that.'

'Noted,' said Liam. 'Pearce, you ready?'

'I was born ready,' said Pearce.

'Good,' said Liam and handed him the map. 'After you.'

To the untrained eye, the dead-letter drop was utterly invisible – which was the whole idea. There was no point in having a secret place stashed with kit or intelligence if it had flashing lights and sirens. Liam knew they could have easily missed it if they hadn't known its exact position and what to look for.

In between two small acacia trees, and concealed beneath a layer of branches and twigs, the drop consisted of a well-hidden hole that was just deep enough to contain ration packs, water and SD cards for the SLR. Liam and Pearce quickly stashed the INT they'd collected, then weighed themselves down with the supplies.

'So this is what it's like to weigh as much as Biggsy,' said Pearce, hoisting his bergen onto his back ready for the trek back to the OP.

Liam did the same. 'I'll take point,' he said.

'Good,' replied Pearce. 'Because, if I'm honest, I just can't be arsed.'

Liam set off, Pearce a few paces behind.

The night was at its blackest now and, as Liam trudged onwards, at times it seemed as though nature was conspiring against them. Branches reached out to snag their kit as they went past, and brush hooked at their ankles to trip them up. Wildlife that woke to the light of the moon could be heard all around. Every couple of hundred paces Liam stopped to check his navigation. Getting lost out here was dangerous not just for him, but for the rest of his section. So he'd check the map against his compass, and then cross-reference that with what he could see in the sky above and any land-marks he'd picked out that he was aiming for. The paces were measured out courtesy of a length of olive-coloured paracord, on which were threaded twenty black beads. For every ten steps, he would flick one through his fingers, all the way up to two hundred paces. It worked a little like a Catholic rosary, though Liam had yet to use it for prayer.

About an hour into their hike back, Pearce called out. 'RB – you sure this is the right route?'

Liam laughed. It was typical of Pearce to mess with his head. 'No, I'm not,' he answered. 'I'm getting us lost on purpose.'

'That would explain why I don't recognize this bit then.'

Liam stopped, checked the map. 'We're here,' he said, pointing out their position to Pearce. 'Another hour and we'll be back.'

Pearce studied the map. 'Look, mate,' he said, 'I'm not being funny, but this doesn't feel right. We should've hit a rise by now, but we're still on the flat.'

Liam checked the map again. 'No, we're definitely right,' he said. 'We're just walking slower, that's all. We came down with empty bags, and now we're carrying a shedload on our backs. That's all.'

Pearce grunted.

Setting off again, Liam was a little pissed off. Pearce was a gruff bastard most of the time, but suggesting that he didn't know what he was doing was out of line. Perhaps he was just trying to rile him?

Fifteen minutes later, when Liam checked again, he started to think that Pearce had a point.

'What's up, RB?'

'Nothing. I mean . . .' Liam's voice faded. He was staring at the map, checking the night sky. Something was wrong.

'You've got us fucking well lost, haven't you, you dozy bastard?'

'Just give me a minute,' said Liam.

'Bollocks to that,' Pearce snapped. 'If we're lost, then we don't have a minute. And wandering around with fuck all clue which direction we need to head in isn't going to help. Give me the map.' He reached out and grabbed it from Liam.

'There's no need to be a dick about it!' Liam snapped, gripping the map even tighter.

'I'm not being a dick,' said Pearce. 'So grow some, will you, and give me the fucking map!' He tugged hard and it eventually came free of Liam's hand.

'We're not lost,' said Liam. 'We're just not exactly where we're supposed to be.'

Pearce shook his head. 'And if that's not the biggest pile of double-talking shite I've ever heard then I don't know what is.'

Liam forced himself to stay calm. But it wasn't easy. Like Pearce, all he wanted now was just to get back to the OP. And arguing wasn't going to help matters.

'Well?' said Liam. 'Where are we then?' He knew he sounded churlish, but he was knackered, grubby and starving. The earlier contact hadn't helped either. His nerves were still on edge.

'I haven't the faintest fucking idea, RB,' said Pearce.

Liam swallowed his pride and leaned in to stare at the map. 'We're supposed to be there,' he said, laying a finger on the line they were meant to be following.

'*Supposed to be* is no fucking good,' said Pearce. 'Either we are or we aren't. And it looks like we aren't.'

Liam's gut twisted hard into a knot. 'You can't be serious.'

'I think we went wrong about a click back,' said Pearce. 'We've wandered off left down this section here when we should be heading up a rise, then veering right.'

Liam sensed the thin claws of panic start to scratch at the back of his neck, pushing up into his brain. 'Biggs will have my balls.'

'It's not Biggsy we have to worry about,' said Pearce. 'If we're still out here in daylight, we'll have to dig a scrape and hope no Al Sha-fucking-baab stumble by.'

Neither Liam nor Pearce said a word for the next couple of minutes as they both studied the map. Pearce checked and double-checked their position with his compass, cross-referencing it with the lay of the land around them.

'You should learn to use one of these,' he said, holding the compass up in front of Liam's face. 'Pretty fucking useful if you want to find your way from one place to another. Come on – we need to head back. If we can find the dead-letter drop again, at least we'll know where we are and get our bearings straight.'

Liam couldn't believe what he was hearing. 'But if we do that we'll be wasting time!' he said. 'We'll have no chance of making it back before sun-up!'

'Well, we'd better just suck it up and get moving,' said Pearce. 'You got enough water in your camel bak?'

'Definitely,' said Liam.

'Good,' said Pearce. 'Because you're going to need it.'

10

Odull's grin was enough to crack even Pearce's grouchy persona.

'Well, fuck me if it isn't Odull, the happiness fairy,' the Geordie corporal said, as Liam and the rest of the section slipped out from where they had been hiding just a few metres away from the edge of the track. Darkness was giving way to dawn, but the sun had as yet not broken the horizon.

'Did I just see you smile?' asked Cordner.

'Make the most of it,' said Pearce. 'It won't last.'

Odull quickly ushered them all into the back of the truck that had taxied them out to the same point six days ago.

'Hard to believe, but I reckon this journey back is going to seem comfortable compared with that army hotel we just left,' said Waterman. The other four-man section had met them back at the original drop-off point.

This time, Liam allowed the others to clamber in first, before squeezing himself in at the last minute. He didn't fancy being all squashed up at the front by the driver's cabin, and instead wanted to be closer to some proper fresh air. Their subsurface observation hole had, he was convinced, almost destroyed his sense of smell. And as for his sense of taste, well, the army had done away with that since he joined Recce and began living on cold ration packs.

'You look well, Lance Corporal Scott,' said Odull, as he lifted the tailgate.

'Don't talk bollocks,' Liam replied. 'We all look like a crock of shit.'

Odull laughed. 'No, you look like that too,' he said. 'But at least you are alive!'

'If this is alive, then being dead must be fecking terrible,' Cordner quipped as Odull dropped the hood.

As the truck swung round and headed back the way it had come, Liam reflected on all that had gone on since leaving the FOB. They'd been lucky. The close call with the Al Shabaab weedheads could have turned nasty, and his cock-up with the navigation . . . it wasn't even worth thinking about. Once they were back and had had a chance to hose themselves down and get some proper grub and rest, he was going to make time to gen up on what could have cost him his life.

Back at the FOB, some of the other sections had already returned, and a few others were still due to come in. Working almost on autopilot, Liam got himself into human form once again, ridding himself of his filthy kit, showering and donning clean clothes. Despite his weariness, he cracked on with sorting his equipment, cleaning his weapons and making sure everything was in place for whatever happened next. At last, with everything done, he collapsed down in the dorm and passed out, the exhaustion of the last few days finally washing over him in a tidal wave.

The next morning, Liam was sitting on his camp bed inside one of a number of shelters erected by the KDF, hunched over his map like a bear tucking into a picnic. After breakfast he'd been true to his word and got straight on with practising his map- and compass-reading skills. He'd also checked through his notes on star navigation. The nights out here were fully dark and the stars were bright and clear. Being able to use them to navigate was something Liam had never really considered before. But now he understood just how essential such skills were. He was still kicking himself for the error he'd made with Pearce after the dead-letter drop.

A head poked in. 'Got a minute, RB?' It was Sergeant Biggs.

'What is it?' Liam asked.

'Owusu has ordered CTRs on a number of key targets. He's asked me to get my team together.'

'What about Waterman's lot?'

'They're a man down,' Biggs replied. 'Fish has managed to get some kind of foot infection. You should see it, mate; like something out of a Rob Zombie movie. Anyway, they're not too gutted. They'll be put to good use by Young, I'm sure.'

'You've spoken to Cordner and Pearce?'

'They're waiting for us,' Biggs said. 'So put your revision notes away, and follow me.'

'I was just—' began Liam, but Biggs cut him off.

'I know what you were just,' he said. 'And I'm impressed. But don't go beating yourself up over what happened. Everyone's fucked up a night nav. It's easy to do and you've learned from it. And because of that it won't happen again.'

Liam said nothing more and followed Biggs over to where Cordner and Pearce were sitting on a couple of camp stools, gobbling slop from mess tins – Cordner's covered in lashings of Tabasco.

'Amazingly,' said Cordner, 'I'd forgotten that this shit actually doesn't taste too bad if it's heated through.'

He held the container up to Liam, who took it from him and munched some of it down himself.

Cordner was right – it was positively delicious.

'Right,' said Biggs, 'this is what we've been tasked with . . .'

He crouched down and unfolded a map of the area they'd just come from, pinning it to the ground with some rocks.

'They're sending us back?' said Pearce. 'What the fuck for?'

'We're not going to the same location exactly,' said Biggs. 'We're heading along here instead.' His finger traced a line along the ridge, then down into the valley. 'The movement we observed at our subsurface hole, well, it seems that it all leads down to this point here.' He tapped his finger on the map. 'One of the other sections found a camp and they want us to get a closer look.'

'There's more to it than that, though, isn't there?' said Pearce. 'CTR means they've spotted something specific and want it confirmed.'

'Absolutely,' said Biggs. 'Seems that Al Shabaab's poster boy was identified in a snap taken by one of the other teams. We're going in to confirm it actually is Abdul Azeez.'

'Just us?' asked Cordner.

'No,' said Biggs, shaking his head. 'We'll be taking four of the Kenyans in with us. Cordner – you and Pearce will go in together, and Scott, you're with me.'

News that they were taking Kenyans in had them all frowning.

'They've had their training, fair enough,' said Pearce, 'but this is some serious shit you're asking of them. And of us too, actually.'

'The lads we're taking are switched on,' said Biggs. 'Wouldn't be coming with us if they were anything else.' He turned then, and gave a signal.

Liam looked over his shoulder. Walking towards them was Odull, and beside him were three other Kenyans.

'All right, lads?' said Biggs when they arrived.

Odull nodded. 'We are ready, Sergeant,' he said, then addressed Liam and the others. 'This is Amaziah Jalloh, Moses Mensah and Obama Okeke. They are good men.'

'The President's man as well,' said Pearce, winking at Obama.

'Sadly, it is a very common name,' said Okeke. 'But I am much better-looking.' That brought a laugh as Okeke beamed a bright white smile.

'Jalloh and Mensah, you will be with Cordner and Pearce. Odull and Okeke, you will be with me and Scott. We will be heading off in two hours,' said Biggs. 'That gives us all enough time to get sorted. We'll meet back here in ninety.'

As Liam made his way back to his bed to go

through his kit once again, Odull caught his shoulder. 'I am glad it is you I am with,' he said.

'Me too, Odull,' Liam said truthfully. Standing beside Odull, he felt like Jack must have done when he confronted the giant. How could they be anything other than successful with him on their side? It was almost guaranteed. And with what they were about to do, a CTR on one of Al Shabaab's most wanted, any kind of guarantee was welcome.

The trip back into Somalia was a serious case of déjà vu. Same truck, same track, same numb backside. Once dropped off, the section made its way along the route Liam and the others had taken a few days earlier. But a few kilometres in, they deviated from the path and trekked into thicker vegetation. In places the way was slow, and Odull and the other Kenyans took point and cut the way through with machetes, which they handled with consummate ease. Liam had used one himself, but was happy to let someone else do the work. They were razor sharp and made swift work of anything in their way. To use one well and without risk to self or others took a lot of practice.

With the last part of their journey ahead, and day about to break the dull gun-metal grey of dawn, the section rested up, swiftly digging scrapes and getting themselves hidden. Then, when night crept back once again, they split into two teams, and Liam, with Biggs, Odull and Okeke, started to make his way down towards their target.

The sergeant halted the group. Voice hushed, he beckoned them around him. 'This is where we are,' he said, shining a small green light onto his map, which was inside a protective waterproof cover. The light came from inside a rubber container hung round his neck with black paracord, and was emitted by a radioactive chemical which would carry on glowing and proving useful for anything up to twenty-five years. It gave off just enough light to allow navigation, but a few steps away would not be noticed. 'From here on in we go slow and panther-quiet. RB?'

Liam looked up at the sergeant.

'You're on point and leading us in.'

Liam made to protest, but Biggs stilled him with a steely glare.

'Night nav is freshest in your mind, so no arguing. It will be down to you when we split into point, relay and fire support. Understood?'

Liam gave an unconvincing nod.

'When you head forward, you'll leave most of your kit with me and Okeke. Odull will follow you in just far enough to act as a relay between you and us. Slip forward, get as close as you can, and get eyes on the target. You've no SLR, so this will be down to your observations only. We'll be in touch on the PRR, but keep comms to a minimum. Then, when you've got enough, fall back to Odull, then to us, and we'll scoot.'

'No problem,' said Liam, doing his best to speak the words with conviction.

'Excellent,' said Biggs, and handed Liam the map. 'Then after you, Lance Corporal.'

Liam didn't speak a word as he started to lead the team down into the valley below. He trusted that they would step where he stepped, so focused instead on every move he was making, ensuring as best as he could that he was silent as a ghost.

An hour later, his body aching from moving so deliberately slowly, Liam heard a new sound slipping towards them from the darkness ahead: voices. He decided this was as good a place as any to drop his kit with Biggs and Okeke. They would be within earshot of the camp, so if something did kick off, and if, for whatever reason, he wasn't able to get a signal back to them, they would know anyway.

'Be proper careful about this from now on,' said Biggs, taking Liam's bergen. 'You're there to observe and that's all. You keep hidden and you stay safe. If anything strikes you as out of the ordinary or a potential threat, you tell me.'

Liam saw that Odull was waiting for him. 'Come on then, Odull,' he said. 'Time to be sneaky little fuckers. Though in your case, we'll forget about the little.'

For once, Odull didn't smile, instead waiting for Liam to pass by before he crept off after him.

It wasn't long before the voices grew clear enough to make out words, not that Liam understood what they were saying. Back in Afghanistan, he'd done pretty well at learning the local dialect up in the Yakchal Valley, but he knew not a single word of Somali. It didn't matter – it wasn't what they were saying that mattered so much as what they were doing, how many of them there were, what weapons and transport they had. That's what Owusu and the KDF wanted to know.

A few metres further on, Liam held up a hand, signalling for Odull to stop. He pointed at the ground and Odull nodded, dropping to his knee.

With Odull now in situ, Liam crept forward, slow and steady, careful to make sure his movement was undetectable. After moving in a half-crouch, almost as though he was crawling through an invisible tunnel, he dropped to a leopard crawl. It was slower, and generally more painful, but it kept his profile low and even more difficult to spot. The ground beneath him did its best to prod and jab and snag him with every move he made, but eventually he came to a point where, any further, he would have been out in the open. And with some of the militants little more than five metres away, that was something Liam was definitely going to avoid.

The camp before him was a freshly cleared area at the bottom of the valley. A few trees had been felled, but most had been left standing, giving good cover from being observed from above. Dotted around were makeshift huts built from whatever the Al Shabaab militants had found around them, including rusting pieces of corrugated iron, plastic sheeting and, on one hut, even an old car door. He could see no track suitable for a vehicle, so his initial assessment was that anyone there had arrived by foot.

The camp was busy and lit everywhere by flaming torches, small fires and candles. These light sources were enough for him to see what was happening, and whatever was going on, it was causing a lot of excitement.

Liam pulled out a notebook and, from his hiding place, started writing everything down. He included the numbers of personnel and their ages. They were all men, and to his relief there were none that looked like children, though he could not guarantee that some of the fighters weren't in their mid-teens. He noted weaponry, most of which comprised numerous AK47s in various states of repair. A few of the men had, to his surprise, American AR15s, but they were definitely in the minority. He also saw a number of crates under a shelter a little way off. What they contained he wasn't sure, but he doubted very much it was someone's order from Amazon. More than likely it was ammunition, RPGs, or both.

Liam stayed low, still and silent for a good two hours, observing everything he could. When he could see no advantage in lying so close to danger any longer, he started to back out, away from the camp. It was then, as he made to leave, that he heard the shouting.

Liam's first thought was that he'd been spotted. He lay still and silent as the dead, listening out for anything that would mean his position had been compromised. Then he saw a group of men being marched into the camp at gunpoint. Flipping down his night vision was no help, the light from the fires blurring the image, so he had to make do with what he'd been born with. Squinting, he waited until the men were closer and easier to make out to confirm exactly who they were and what they were about.

Initially he thought they were just another group of Al Shabaab terrorists come to join in the fun. Then he realized it was something very different. The new arrivals were all wearing military fatigues and were stumbling, badly wounded. Hands tied and blindfolded, they were kicked and pushed and thumped with each step they took. Al Shabaab men prodded them with the barrels of their weapons, spat at them, pushed them onto the ground only so that they could beat them, heave them back to their feet, then do the same again.

Liam froze. He knew immediately who they were: the KDF soldiers kidnapped from BATUK a few weeks ago. There were five men in total, each in a bad way, and all displaying signs of ill-treatment and malnourishment. Then another thought struck him hard: if he was right, then one of them was Odull's brother.

Liam buzzed Biggs on the PRR. 'They've got the Kenyan hostages,' he whispered very softly. 'Five of them. Look beaten to fuck.'

Biggs came back on the PRR immediately. 'Get the fuck out of there now, Scott. No messing around. Whatever you've got is enough. Move it!'

Liam was about to do just that when the KDF hostages were forced onto their knees in the centre of the camp. They looked terrified. Around them, men were cheering and shouting. Then, from one of the huts further away, a figure emerged onto the scene. He was tall – Liam guessed around six foot – and compared to the others, his clothes were almost clean. The dirt of Somalia was barely visible on his white shalwar kameez, which made Liam think that this was a man who travelled more by vehicle than on foot. His beard was long and well trimmed, and he stroked it like someone would a pet. He was armed too, but unlike everyone else, he was holding with pride an American SCAR. Liam had no doubt that this had been taken from one of the soldiers. He also recognized the new arrival.

'Azeez's here!' he hissed down the PRR.

'That's all we need to know,' replied Biggs. 'Now get your arse back here!'

Liam hesitated. 'What about the hostages?'

'Nothing we can do.'

'You mean leave them?'

'This is not a rescue operation, Scott. We'd be shredded.'

Liam watched as Abdul Azeez moved through the circle of men and towards the blindfolded hostages on the ground. He was smiling as though this was the best goddamned day of his life. It was chilling and the hairs on Liam's arms bristled in response.

'Scott . . .'

Azeez walked round the hostages, slapping the shoulders of the men surrounding them, laughing, cheering. Then he stopped and moved in close. He crouched down next to one of the KDF soldiers and leaned in, whispering. The hostage didn't respond, was probably too terrified to do anything, thought Liam. Then Azeez stood up, pointed his rifle, and fired.

11

The crack of the bullet shattered the silence and Liam saw the dead soldier fall to the ground, the back of his head missing and now splattered in pieces across the ground. The other hostages started screaming, but that was soon drowned out by more cheering, which jostled in the air with weapons fired in celebration.

Liam was caught by the shock of what he'd just witnessed. He'd seen death plenty of times and in plenty of ways, but something so cold-blooded made him shudder. Vomit stung the back of his throat, but he swallowed it back down, the taste and the sting of it making his eyes water. He stared as Azeez continued to smile, then walked casually up to the soldier's body to kick it before finally emptying the rest of his rifle's magazine into his chest.

Liam knew he had to get out of there, and fast. But he couldn't just up and run. He was so close that any rapid movement would be spotted and investigated. And having seen the way prisoners were dealt with, being discovered was not an option.

With deliberate slowness, his eyes still focused on the hideous scene playing out before him, Liam backed off. Reverse leopard crawl was awkward, and with every move his body complained, not just with the knocks and bruises, but with the stress of having to make every inch gained silent and invisible. Every sound he made seemed to be amplified horribly. Yet Liam didn't stop, couldn't. He had to get back to the others.

At last, Odull loomed out of the darkness, the big Kenyan moving along the direction Liam had taken to get to the terrorist camp.

'I heard the shot,' he said, his voice a stern whisper. 'I thought the worst, and was coming to—'

'We need to move,' Liam whispered, cutting Odull off, and indicating with a nod of his head to turn round and head back to the sergeant and Okeke. 'There's nothing to see.'

'What happened?' Odull asked, his voice low, quiet and bristling. Liam could tell he was gunning for a fight. 'Did they see you? Who fired?'

Liam didn't have time to explain. 'Just move it!' he hissed. 'And that's an order!'

Liam pushed past and heard Odull fall in behind

him. He didn't want to say what he'd seen – not right now, at any rate. Odull was a top-notch soldier, but news of his brother could push his loyalties too far. Learning that one of the hostages had been murdered would only add to that pressure. What if the soldier Azeez had so casually executed *was* Odull's brother? Liam didn't want to risk telling him something that would send him racing off to a brave, glorious but undoubtedly pointless death.

When they came up to Biggs and were at a safe enough distance from the camp to talk, Biggs was into Liam immediately.

'What the living *fuck* is going on, Scott?' he hissed through clenched teeth. 'I told you to get out. You hesitated. Explain.'

'Abdul Azeez,' said Liam, not giving the sergeant chance to take a breath. 'He killed one of the hostages. Just picked one at random and took him out. No warning or anything. Point blank with a SCAR. Nigh on took his head off. Enjoyed it too, the bastard.'

Odull and Okeke bristled at the news.

'The hostages? Then my brother is there also! Was it him they killed?'

'There were five,' said Liam. 'Azeez killed one of them on the spot, like I said. The others, I don't know. I heard no more—'

'What did he look like, the man who was shot?' Odull interrupted.

'I don't know.'

'You must then remember,' said Odull, pushing for answers. 'My brother is smaller than me, slim. He has a mark here from an accident as a child when he fell from a tree.' He traced a line across the right of his own head. 'Hair does not grow there now. You would have noticed!'

'All I noticed,' said Liam, 'was some proper fucking nutjob with a SCAR slotting a KDF soldier in cold blood and getting a fucking buzz out of it! The other bastards with him were all cheering and dancing like it was the best thing that could've happened!'

'But was it my brother?'

Odull's voice was raised and Biggs stepped in, shutting him down on the spot.

'We can't do anything about it,' he said. 'There's four of us. We have no backup. We can't go in, and neither are we authorized to do so. We'd be shot to pieces, and the hostages as well.'

'He was wearing a blindfold, but I didn't see a mark,' said Liam, pausing to remember. 'The one who was shot – there was no mark.'

Odull still didn't relax.

'Enough chinwag,' said Biggs. 'Azeez's presence is

confirmed, and the sighting of the hostages is good additional INT. We now get back sharpish. Those fuckers are trigger-happy and finding us would only add to their fun. Let's move out!'

They arrived back at the FOB early the following morning, after hiding away during daylight hours.

The atmosphere at the base was all anticipation and impatience – Liam could taste it in the air, a mix of sweat, hot air, dust: the telltale signs of soldiers at work. Not one person was at rest, with everyone racing around the site collecting and sorting equipment, being pulled over for meetings, checking maps, cleaning weapons.

With all the INT that he and the rest of Recce Platoon had collected, there was no doubt in anyone's mind that it was only a matter of hours before the KDF went in. But what had really got everyone on a red alert was his own confirmation of the presence of Abdul Azeez and the hostages. That one of them had been killed already had sent a wave of bloodlust through the KDF troops. The hostages weren't just other soldiers, they were mates, and as a soldier himself Liam utterly understood their compulsion not only to rescue their friends, but also to take the fight to the enemy.

After resting up from the CTR, he was throwing some food down his neck in the temporary mess canteen set up by the KDF. Soldiers buzzed in, did the same, and were quickly out again. There was no time to savour the food. It was fuel, nothing more. Sitting around him were the rest of the section, even Fish with his rotting foot.

'You should smell it when he takes his sock off,' said Waterman. 'It's like puke and guts and shit, all rolled into one.'

'You forgot pus,' said Fish. 'It's got a hint of that in there too.'

'So you stuck here, then?' Liam asked.

'No choice,' Fish told him. 'I walk like a zombie in *Day of the Dead* with this thing. No way can I chase down Al Shabaab for a party.'

'Just seen Lieutenant Young talking to the captain,' said Waterman. 'I reckon kickoff is only a couple of hours away – as soon as it gets dark again.'

'Hope so,' said Pearce. 'Sitting around is bollocks.'

Biggs reached over and snatched a piece of toast from Liam's tray.

'Help yourself.'

'I did.'

'You spoken to Odull?'

Liam shook his head.

'The big man took himself off. He's gone quiet. It's unnerving. He wants his brother back. Knowing we were so close will be ripping his insides apart.'

*   *   *

Early that evening, when Recce Platoon were called together and briefed on what was going to happen next, Liam caught sight of Odull, but there was no response. He couldn't guess at the pain and frustration the man would be feeling. He also wondered if Odull blamed him for not allowing him to go in to rescue his brother.

But they'd had no choice. Liam knew if he hadn't waited until they were with Biggs before mentioning the hostages, then there was a good chance Odull would've gone in and got himself killed in the process.

Captain Owusu got straight to the point. 'Our mission statement is to lead the KDF on to the location where Abdul Azeez is, we hope, still holed up. We'll be sending two sections in as their eyes and ears, advancing ahead of the main army and guiding them in. The rest will stay back in a support role. As the KDF attacks, flares will be sent up. We stay and observe, report what we see, then head back when the time is right to do so.'

'We're one of the sections, by the way,' said Biggs to Liam and the others. 'Fish is hanging back and is being replaced by another lad, Sam Carter. I chose him. Top soldier, trust me.'

'Back we go again, then,' said Pearce. 'Might as well put an offer in and buy a bit of land there, build myself a nice little holiday home.'

'What about the hostages?' asked a soldier at the back of the group.

'We can't risk a rescue as such,' said Owusu. 'Not only do we not know if they're still being held at that location, we don't even know if the rest are still alive. Abdul Azeez killed one. He could have killed the others by now. We cannot risk lives on a possibility. If they are alive, then we will endeavour to release them as part of this operation.'

What worried Liam, though, was that once the KDF engaged with Al Shabaab, anyone caught in the crossfire wouldn't stand a chance.

By midnight, Liam was once again eyes on the camp at which he'd carried out the CTR. In addition to their personal weapons, which were there for protection rather than for direct engagement, they also had the SLR and spotting scope. Cordner was responsible for the main radio and keeping in regular contact with the FOB. They all still had PRRs to communicate with each other and the rest of their section.

'We should start a business when we get back home,' said Pearce, gesturing to their newly-dug scrape. 'Holes are always needed, right? We'd make millions.'

Liam smiled, but didn't pull away from the scope. Now, between their subsurface observation post and the

Al Shabaab camp, the KDF were advancing slowly and carefully. And considering there were nearly 200 of them, they were proving difficult to spot. Of that he was glad – everyone wanted the op to go smoothly. A prolonged and bloody fight out here was not a part of the plan. The rest of Recce Platoon were positioned to the left and right of where Liam, Pearce, Biggs and Cordner were holed up, all relaying INT back to Captain Owusu.

'Did you see how wired some of them were?' asked Cordner.

'That'll be the khat,' said Biggs.

'Can't believe they're allowed to take it,' said Pearce. 'Imagine if we all dropped a few "E"s before engaging? We'd all be too busy raving and talking ratshit fast!'

'Khat's legal,' Biggs pointed out.

'It's crazy, is what it is,' said Pearce. 'Anyway, RB, how's it looking out there?'

'Quiet,' Liam replied. 'They're closing in. Nothing from the terrorists. The camp is dead.'

'You mean empty?'

'No,' said Liam. 'There's movement, but nothing like I observed. Probably all asleep.'

'If the KDF do this right,' said Biggs, 'and catch the terrorists in their beds, then we should be out of here pretty soon. Of course, the most important word there is *if* . . .'

Liam wondered how Odull was doing. He was down there somewhere, heading to where he knew his brother was being held, and keeping his head straight and his mind on the job under that kind of pressure would be more than difficult.

'The KDF are getting ready for the attack,' said Liam.

'Sure?' asked Biggs.

'Definitely,' said Liam. 'All movement has stopped. They're in position and waiting for the ref to blow his whistle.'

For the next couple of minutes, not one of them spoke. Though they weren't down at the sharp end of the coming battle, they were a part of it, and knew the dangers facing the lads about to go in. They had the element of surprise, and that would play to their advantage, but beyond that, luck always had a say in how things would pan out. Liam just hoped it was text-book, and any resistance encountered was both weak and dealt with swiftly.

Rifle fire rattled them all from their thoughts.

'The fuck is that?'

Liam tried to pinpoint it. Couldn't.

'The flare's not gone up yet!' snarled Biggs. 'Who's firing?'

'Can't see!' said Liam.

'Fucking well look harder, then!'

More weapons were let loose, and in a heartbeat the silence of the valley was shattered by the sound of rifle fire.

Then bright lights burst in the sky, scorching the land below in a yellowy glow, as flares floated down on tiny parachutes, like fiery angels falling to Earth.

12

The crack and thump of rifle fire ripped at the night, clawing at the silence and shredding it. Darkness was sliced by tracer fire as below Liam the KDF engaged with Al Shabaab.

'Cordner!' ordered Biggs, his voice quiet but a rasp betraying his desperation to yell. 'Get on that fucking radio and find out what the hell is going on!'

'I'm already on it,' said Cordner, pinning his headset to his ear to block out as much external noise as possible. 'Nothing confirmed. Only that fighting broke out early.'

'And what do they want us to do about it? Just sit and watch?'

'Keep eyes on,' Cordner reported back. 'We're not to engage unless absolutely necessary.'

'And what the bollocking hell is the definition of absolutely necessary?' asked Pearce, teeth clenched.

'When one of us gets our knackers shot off?'

'Wind your neck in!' said Biggs. 'You know damned well we can't go wading into that shit storm!'

'But they're getting cut to pieces!' said Pearce.

'Holy fuck!' said Liam. 'It's opening up all over the place!'

The telltale sound of rounds thumping into the ground around them made them all flinch.

'It can't be!' Biggs hit back. 'There's only us and the KDF out here, and Al Shabaab are down in that camp!'

'I'm serious!' said Liam. 'There's small arms fire all over the place!' He scanned left and right. Muzzle flashes were coming from everywhere now, not just advancing on the camp below either, but spreading outwards and, most unnervingly, up towards them.

Biggs jumped up on the other scope. 'Christ, they're everywhere! It's a bloody ambush!'

'That would mean they knew the KDF were coming!' Liam replied, and the thought was terrifying. It was one thing to go into battle prepared for most eventualities. But an ambush was a worst-case scenario.

More rounds came in, peppering the ground above them.

'So how long are we going to sit here before we bugger off?' asked Pearce.

'They won't know our exact positions,' said Liam. 'Only we know that, right? We're safe for the moment, surely.'

'Can't guarantee anything with that shit storm blowing in,' said Biggs.

A voice crackled through on the PRR. It was Waterman. 'We're thinking this isn't exactly what the captain had in mind.'

'Well, a round of applause for Miss Marple,' said the sergeant.

Just then an explosion hammered the ground, sending a ripple of shock waves through the hole.

'That was a fucking mortar!' Biggs yelled. 'Either some nutjob is letting them off for a laugh, or they actually *do* know where we fucking well are! Scott – you got eyes on that?'

Liam scanned, saw dust and smoke rising from the ground below them. 'Ten o'clock, two hundred metres,' he said.

Cordner was on the radio again, and Liam heard him yell, 'Are we staying put, or getting the feck out?' Then his face stilled. Something was wrong. 'It gets worse,' he said, turning to face the others. 'Just come in that one of the KDF lads switched sides.'

'Oh, fuck . . .' said Biggs.

'That would explain the mortar,' said Liam. 'And I

147

don't know about anyone else, but I don't fancy waiting around for them to get any closer.'

'Christ knows how he got away with it,' said Cordner. 'But they reckon he was basically a sleeper. Loyal to Al Shabaab and just waiting for the right moment to do his bit.'

'And this was it?' said Liam. 'Well, that's just fucking brilliant! What the hell happened?'

'When the KDF were within spitting distance of the terrorist camp, he opened up on the guys around him, then made a run for it. Five casualties confirmed.'

Another mortar round came in.

'Ten o'clock, one-fifty!' said Liam and ducked instinctively as it slammed another shock wave through the ground. 'They're trying to get a range on us. We need to move!'

Biggs rounded on Cordner. 'You tell those bastards at the FOB we need to fuck right off, and I mean now! If one of the KDF was Al Shabaab, then there's every chance they know our positions! And I'm not going to have us waiting around like a bunch of bloody tourists!'

'The fighting is definitely moving up towards us,' said Liam. 'I reckon the KDF are trying to fight their way out, but it's not looking good. We need to shift.'

Biggs called Waterman on the PPR. 'You got anything from the FOB?'

'Our radio's playing up,' he said. 'Can't get through. Still trying.'

'Then sod this for a game of soldiers,' said Biggs, and was back to Cordner. 'Use that Irish charm of yours and tell them we've got incoming – mortars, small arms fire. And that we're extracting now.'

'They won't be happy,' said Cordner.

'Well, I'll just have to wear my jester's outfit later to cheer them the fuck up, won't I?' replied Biggs. 'We're moving!'

Another mortar, this one close enough to rain muck and smashed plant remains down on the four men. Then shouting from either side of the scrape.

'Confirm who the hell that is – *NOW!*' Biggs yelled at Liam.

Liam fully understood the sergeant's concern. With the KDF now actively engaged with Al Shabaab, the last thing they needed was to find themselves in live contact with the wrong target. A blue on blue had to be avoided at all costs.

He saw movement. Three men were approaching.

'Nine o'clock, one hundred,' he said. 'Not KDF.'

'Positive?'

Despite the darkness, Liam could see that the men were dressed in little more than T-shirts and baggy trousers.

'Confirmed,' said Liam.

'Pearce! Cordner!'

The two soldiers were up at the side of the hole as more rounds came in.

'Take those fuckers down!' yelled Biggs. 'Now!'

Pearce and Cordner opened fire as Waterman called in on the PRR, 'They're coming out like rats escaping a fucking flood!' he said.

Liam dropped down as a burst of rounds took the scope apart, showering them all with glass and shrapnel.

'We fall back now,' said Biggs. 'Scott, you're with me. Pearce – you and Cordner cover us as we move out. Fire manoeuvre all the way and no getting shot! An injury now is the last thing we need.'

Liam scrambled over to Biggs. 'Not quite the day I had in mind,' he said, readying his weapon.

'All part of the fun,' Biggs replied. 'Pearce? Cordner? Cover! Now!'

As Pearce and Cordner opened fire, Liam and the sergeant heaved themselves out of their hole. Liam dropped to his knee, fired, and Biggs raced on past him. Then he was up and past Biggs, who was now doing the same. Rounds peppered the ground about them, and eventually they both dropped into a dip behind a fallen tree.

Moments later, as they laid down covering fire, Pearce and Cordner slid in beside them.

'We're in the shit,' said Liam, breathing hard.

'I've changed my mind about buying land out here,' said Pearce. 'Don't think the locals like me.'

'Mate, Jesus probably has a job liking you,' said Liam.

'Jesus thinks I'm a fucking sunbeam,' replied Pearce.

'You should have that on your gravestone,' Liam told him.

'If it's all the same with everyone here,' said Pearce, 'I'd rather not put an order in for one quite yet.'

Liam hushed everyone. 'Voices,' he said and pointed the way they were heading, then got himself on his knees and was looking down his rifle through his ACOG. Beside him Pearce was doing the same. Biggs and Cordner were scanning both flanks.

The voices were accompanied by the sound of people crunching through the undergrowth. Either they were sure no one was around to hear them, or they were overly confident in their own indestructibility.

'Can't be any of our lot,' whispered Liam. 'Not making a noise like that.'

About twenty metres in front of them, a group of armed shadows appeared. It was clear that they were Al Shabaab from the way they were dressed in baggy tunics and trousers, their AL47s slung low in their hands. Then one of them saw Liam and the others and, shouting, raised his weapon and fired.

The rounds, badly aimed, cut through the dark as Liam and Pearce returned fire, Cordner and Biggs swinging round to back them up. The terrorist who had opened fire first dropped to the ground like a felled tree. His mates, seemingly stunned to have met resistance, backed away quickly, firing from the hip, and were gone almost as quickly as they'd arrived.

Liam turned to the others. 'They're everywhere,' he said. 'The place is crawling with them.'

'That's not our biggest problem,' said Cordner, who was now crouched down next to where Biggs was lying.

Their sergeant was face down on the ground, weapon pinned beneath him.

'Was he hit?'

'Don't know,' said Cordner, and raced through the drill to check a man for wounds, running his hands down Biggs's body from head to toe, checking for dampness, the telltale sign of blood seeping from a wound.

'Nothing,' he said. 'We need to roll him.'

Liam was closest and slid over. He looked over at Pearce. 'You keep an eye out, mate. Any more of those bastards come looking for some, you let them have it.'

Pearce didn't reply; there was no need.

Liam helped Cordner lever Biggs gently over onto his side, then onto his back. A hefty bruise was visible on his forehead between the lip of his helmet and his left eyebrow.

'Where the hell did he get that?' Liam asked.

'Only thing I can think of,' said Cordner, 'is that one of the rounds ricocheted a stone up off the ground and it twatted him on the bonce. He's breathing fine, just unconscious.'

'Is he OK to be moved?' Liam asked. 'Not that I want to, the heavy bastard.'

Cordner said, 'Yes. We'll just have to take it in turns. Fireman's lift.'

'I'll go first then,' said Liam. 'Pearce, can you take my bergen? Cordner, Biggsy's?'

Cordner checked the map. 'We've no choice but to just keep making our way back down the way we came out. And we need to get as far as we can before day breaks. The more distance we put between this balls-up and ourselves the better.'

Small arms fire followed immediately after Cordner had stopped speaking.

'Then let's get moving,' said Liam, and slid off his bergen, handing it to Pearce as Cordner helped him with the sergeant.

'Got him?'

Liam nodded as the weight of Biggs on his back seemed to push him down into the ground.

'We can't afford to over-fatigue ourselves,' said Cordner. 'We've only got so much water. So let's be sensible with this. We rush, we'll end up with even more injuries, and then we really will be screwed.'

Liam was immediately conscious of his ankles. If he went down with Biggs on him, they wouldn't just twist – they'd probably snap right off.

'If you take point,' he said to Cordner, 'I can follow, with Pearce behind.'

As they set off, Liam remembered his escape and evasion training back during the LRCC. The adrenaline he'd felt as he'd done his best to not get caught, the fear that had coursed through him when he'd finally been cornered, and the horror of the interrogation. As he fell in behind Cordner, he tried not to think of what would happen to them if Al Shabaab managed to cut them off. One thing was for certain, though: it would make the training seem like child's play.

13

'He's awake.'

The lads were so fired up with adrenaline that they'd barely noticed it was approaching first light. With little time to get to cover, they'd managed against the odds to find a fallen tree to use as shelter. With a bit of work they'd been able to sort the space underneath into a passable hideaway, with Pearce heading back up their trail to rub out their tracks with a broken branch.

Liam looked over to where Biggs was laying. 'How is he?'

'Grumpy,' said Cordner.

'Fuck off,' said Biggs, trying to sit up. 'What happened? My head feels like it's been kicked by a bull.'

'Stay where you are,' ordered Cordner. 'You'll be suffering from concussion. Last thing we need now is you standing up and falling over to twat yourself again.'

'I'm fine,' said Biggs.

'I don't care if you think you can swing through the trees like a fucking baboon, you're not fecking moving.'

Biggs made a poor attempt at an ape impression, then relented and rested his head back on the ground. 'I remember a contact,' he said. 'Now I'm here. Wherever *here* is . . .' He looked around at where they were now encamped. 'Not bad, not bad. Is there hot running water?'

'Sorry, Sarge,' said Liam. 'As to where we are: safe, we hope. You were knocked out by a ricochet,' he explained. 'We've been carrying you since the contact. And when we get back, you need to lose some – you're a fat bastard.'

'Bet that was fun,' said Biggs.

'Start to finish.'

Liam's body was aching all over and he had no doubt that the other two were in just the same condition. He, Cordner and Pearce had taken it in turns to be either point man, Sherpa with the sergeant's kit, or the one unlucky enough to have him on their shoulders. And Biggsy wasn't exactly light.

'What about the enemy?'

'We've managed to stay out of sight so far,' Liam said. 'Heard them, but that's all. Now we have to hide here until it falls dark again. Don't fancy our chances if we have to run in daylight.'

Pearce pushed his way back into the hide. 'Tracks covered,' he said, breathing deeply. 'Only way they'll find us here is by luck – theirs, not ours, of course. And if they do . . .' He patted his rifle.

Liam pulled out the map and spread it on the ground before them. They all leaned in, Biggs slowly easing himself over to rest on a bent arm.

'You know how to use these things now?' asked Pearce.

'This is where we are,' said Liam, ignoring him and marking a point on the map with a finger. 'We move as soon as it's dark. We should make it to the extraction point before the next day breaks. It's only about seven miles away, but we'll be going quiet and careful. Last thing we need is to get pinged by Al Shabaab.'

Pearce leaned in for a closer look. 'Nicely done,' he said, then added, 'If you're not careful, you'll end up a proper soldier. How fucking terrifying.'

'I know,' said Liam. 'But then I've been watching you and making sure I do the exact opposite.'

'You mentioned an extraction point,' said Biggs. 'Someone going to be there to meet us?'

Cordner nodded. 'I've already radioed it in. We'll be the last ones back in.'

'You mean the rest of our section are still out as well?'

Pearce nodded. 'Waterman got caught in a firefight. Delayed them a bit. No casualties on their side, but I don't think the terrorists exactly got away unharmed. They'll be meeting us there. It'll be emotional.'

'So no casualties at all then?' asked Biggs.

'From Recce?' answered Liam. 'You're the closest. As for the KDF . . .' His voice trailed off.

'What about the KDF?' asked Biggs, serious now, eyes drilling into Liam for an answer.

Liam didn't want to give one, but had to. His words came out broken. 'Numbers aren't confirmed yet,' he said. 'But from what we've been told so far, there's over twenty KIA and numerous others injured. The rest are still being picked up and taken back to the FOB.'

'Twenty?' said Biggs, face grave. 'That's fucking horrific. That can't be right.'

'I'm afraid it is,' said Liam. 'And the number could still go up.'

'We should have gone in to help,' said Pearce.

'No, we shouldn't have,' said Biggs. 'It's a terrible loss of life. Adding ours to the list of casualties would be of no use to anyone.'

For a moment everyone was quiet. Being a soldier was inherently dangerous, but for the KDF to lose ten per cent of its men in one night was devastating.

'We'd best get some shuteye then,' said Biggs. 'And before anyone asks, yes, I will be able to walk when we shift it later. And I'll be taking no arguments on that.'

'You won't get any either,' said Pearce. 'Carrying you hasn't exactly been a highlight.'

Liam was first to take watch, allowing the others to collapse quickly into a deep, much needed sleep. The view wasn't ideal, but at least they were out of sight, and he got himself into a position that kept him hidden but still allowed him to survey the land around them. About half an hour into his watch, a herd of impala came to graze in the distance, eventually moving off. Liam was almost sorry to see them go, their absence somehow making his and the rest of the lads' situation even more acute. The sky, a bright sheet of blue hanging above them, was broken only by occasional flocks of birds and far-off clouds. He focused in on the sounds around him, trying to filter through for anything out of the ordinary. He was relieved when it came to his turn to get some shuteye, with Cordner taking his place.

'We still alone, then?'

'Haven't heard a thing,' said Liam, lying down.

'Then let's hope I don't either,' replied Cordner.

Liam was snatched roughly from his sleep by a shake of his shoulder. Pearce was staring at him, finger to his lips. Cordner and Biggs were awake, both with their automatic rifles at the ready.

For a moment Liam couldn't work out what had got Pearce and the others so spooked. Then his head cleared and he heard it. Not just the rustle of movement, but voices.

It was still daylight. Cordner had obviously done his stint on watch, followed by Pearce, who'd woken him.

Biggs caught his attention and signalled to where the noises were coming from. Liam quietly reached for his own weapon. He was fully alert now, forcing his mind to control the fear that wanted him to run for his life.

The voices were moving closer. Listening in, concentrating all his attention on what he could hear, Liam was able to make out at least five individuals. He then watched as Cordner slid silently forward to see if he could get eyes on who was out there. He was back inside the hide sharpish as a single voice shouted out from what was patently just a few metres away.

Shit, thought Liam, they're right on top of us!

Biggs hastily signalled what was to happen next if it kicked off, pointing to Cordner and Pearce to provide cover as he and Liam bugged out from the other side of where they were hiding. Liam knew that he and the sergeant would then quickly find somewhere from where to provide covering fire for the others as they followed behind.

The voice just outside their hideaway shouted out

once more. Liam held his breath, steadied himself. His heart was racing, his palms sweaty. He wasn't sure what was worse, the waiting, or knowing that he could soon be fighting for his life.

They all heard movement as the other voices came closer. And none of them sounded happy in the slightest as what began as raised voices quickly deteriorated into a full-blown argument. Liam guessed they were probably just pissed off to be wandering around trying to find him and the others.

The argument subsided and Liam started to think that perhaps they were going to move away. But then, without warning, it kicked off again, only this time with renewed violence as the telltale sounds of a fist fight broke out. The branches of the fallen tree shook violently as whatever was going on quickly got out of hand. Then, after a sharp yell, a section of the branches gave way and Liam and the others came face to face with one of the pursuers.

At the sight of four armed soldiers in front of him, he yelled and disappeared back out of the branches in a shot. Then Pearce and Cordner went into action and opened fire.

Liam was up and racing out of the other side of the fallen tree, Biggs at his side. The sound of automatic rifles echoed all around them as they both dropped down behind a small clump of bushes. They offered little protection, but Liam ignored that and had his rifle up in the shoulder. He opened up with short three-round bursts, the sergeant alongside him doing the same, as from under the tree came Cordner and Pearce. They kept on with the covering fire as they shot past. When they were clear, Biggs lobbed a phosphorous grenade which exploded into life a couple of seconds later, covering the area in front of them in thick white smoke. Liam then chucked in one of his own. The smoke wouldn't stop the terrorists giving chase, but it would at least confuse them a little as to which direction to follow.

With another burst of fire, Liam made to stand up and go when out of the smoke came two terrorists. Their weapons, both AK47s, were held at their hips, and they were spraying rounds wildly in front of them. Liam took aim and dropped them both. Biggs was up then, and Liam followed as covering fire came in from Cordner and Pearce.

As they skidded in next to them, Pearce said, 'Waterman's just come on the PPR. Wants to know if we need any help.'

'Where are they?' asked Biggs.

Liam was down on his knee, staring out ahead, waiting to see if the terrorists were still going to advance.

'South of here,' said Pearce. 'Not close enough to be of any use, though.'

'Get their position. Tell them we'll rendezvous with them ASAP.'

Pearce nodded, sent the message.

'Everyone up for a nice afternoon stroll?' Biggs asked. 'Pearce, you're on point. Cordner, you're with him. We'll cover and follow. Move!'

Sometime later, Liam was sucking breath in hard and fast when, with Biggs just in front of him, he dropped in over the lip of a small dip in the ground ahead and found himself with the rest of the section.

'Still alive then, RB?' Waterman was looking at him with a grin on his face.

'Best way to be, I reckon,' said Liam. 'Certainly better than the alternative.'

Three soldiers were up at the lip of the rise, weapons at the ready. Two of them he knew, Airey and Bale. The other was the soldier the sergeant had selected to replace Fish, Sam Carter, who had to fight a constant battle with his bright red hair to try and keep it camouflaged.

'We've seen no movement, other than you lot tramping through the place like pissheads out on a Friday night,' said Waterman.

'Scott dropped two,' said Biggs. 'No idea about the rest.'

Liam hadn't had a chance to think about the two men he'd opened fire on. He'd had no choice, as they'd been running at them, weapons firing. And now wasn't the time to dwell on it either. It had been a split-second decision, and the right one.

'So what now?' asked Airey, without taking his eye from where his weapon was aimed.

'It may still be daylight, but I reckon our best bet is to make our way to the extraction point,' said Biggs. 'We'll get there quicker in the light with less risk of tripping up and risking injury, set up a perimeter, and wait it out.' He paused, then said, 'Unless anyone has any more pressing business, that is.'

'I'm all out of jokes,' said Pearce. 'So I reckon we go with your suggestion and get the fuck out of here good and proper.'

The rest of the section muttered their agreement.

'We'll walk this as a patrol,' continued Biggs. 'Nice and steady, no running, no fucking this up so close to getting out. Everyone get their ground sight together, and we'll be fine.'

Liam momentarily zoned out of what the sergeant was saying. He was listening in for any sound of movement from the direction they'd just come from. So far, nothing. But that didn't mean the terrorists weren't out there, and getting closer.

'Let's shift it then,' he said. 'Who's on point?'

Carter slipped down from his viewpoint. 'I'll head it up,' he said. 'Spent most of my last tour doing it with a metal detector, so why change the habit?'

Liam remembered a lad who'd done the same back during his last tour. Point man was supposed to be done on rotation, everyone taking their turn, but he'd been so good everyone was happy just to let him crack on.

And with that, the section headed off, Liam fifth in line.

As they walked, everyone was scanning left and right, hardly a word spoken. The ground was easy going, but acacia trees seemed to reach out to grab them and the long grass snatched at their boots. Every now and again, someone would stop the patrol and they'd drop to their knees, rifles at the ready, barrels aimed left and right. Then they'd carry on, carefully making their way on towards where, soon, a helicopter would come to fetch them.

It was as the day was starting to yawn, the sun slipping away from the land, that the section was halted once again, this time by Waterman.

'What is it?' Liam asked.

Waterman shushed him with a raised hand.

Liam couldn't hear anything, but Waterman

continued to hold the section still. Then Liam heard it too. 'What is that?'

'Sounds like someone in pain,' said Waterman. 'Anyone else getting that?'

The rest of the section focused hard on the noise Waterman had stopped them for.

'Where's it coming from?' asked Parker.

'Nine o'clock from our direction of travel,' said Waterman.

'Definitely sounds human,' said Biggs, and he called the section together. 'Suggestions?'

'Haven't got much choice, have we?' said Waterman. 'If it's one of the terrorists, we bag ourselves a prisoner. If it's one of the KDF, we'll be saving one of the good guys.'

'Agreed,' said Biggs. 'Waterman? You heard it, you take point. You've probably the best bearing on it, OK?'

Waterman nodded and moved out with the rest falling in behind. This time, though, Liam was at the front rather than in the middle, and the sense of being more exposed was tangible. If there was something bad ahead, he and Waterman would face it first.

As they walked on, the noise grew louder and became clearly human. Approximately fifteen minutes later, they found the cause.

'Christ, he looks fucked up,' said Cordner, who was a few steps behind Liam.

The man was in KDF uniform, and even though they were still at a distance, they could tell he was in a bad state. From the way he was lying, one leg was definitely broken; it was twisted the wrong way and buckled like a tree trunk snapped by a storm. He was propped up against a stump, head lolling from side to side as he moaned. The rest of him was covered in a mush of blood and mud and his head looked battered and bruised.

'I don't like it,' said Liam.

'How do you mean?' said Waterman.

'What's he doing here?' Liam said. 'How did he get here? We're nowhere near where it kicked off between the KDF and Al Shabaab. It doesn't feel right.' His sixth sense was on overdrive.

Biggs walked up from the rear. 'What's wrong?'

The man was still moaning, but seemed to Liam to be swinging in and out of consciousness.

'Doesn't smell right,' he said.

'Waterman?'

'I don't know,' said Waterman. 'Scott's right – what the fuck is this dude doing out here like this?'

'You think it's a trap?'

'We need to be seriously fucking cagey about it, is what I think,' said Waterman.

Biggs signalled down the line for everyone to get eyes on to the land around them. 'I'll go in,' he said. 'Carter, you're with me. Scott, cover us. Understood?'

Liam nodded, then watched as the sergeant and Carter started to make their way towards the injured man. They were within a couple of steps of him when two shots rang out. The first shattered the skull of the injured man, killing him instantly. The second dropped Carter like a rag doll.

Then all hell broke loose.

As the area around them was lit up with automatic rifle fire, Liam saw two men race over towards the sergeant, who was down on one knee, covering the injured Carter. Rifle in the shoulder, Liam caught the first in the chest with a three-round burst. The second he hit in the leg, dropping him no less than ten metres from the sergeant. Despite his injuries, the man raised his weapon again, but Biggs was on to him and put him down sharpish.

Liam snapped round to Cordner. 'Cover me!' He didn't give the Irishman a chance to answer, but was on his feet, racing over to Carter. 'Where's he hit?'

'Doesn't matter!' Biggs shouted back. 'It's a fucking ambush! That soldier was smashed up and dropped here to lure us. Now help me grab Carter and let's get the fuck out of here!'

Liam grabbed hold of Carter's right arm and hoisted him up as Biggs grabbed the other arm. Then they were racing across to the rest of the section.

Rounds were buzzing the ground, sending up tiny whirlwinds of dust and dirt, splattering Liam with grit and stones. Normally it would have stung like hell, but he had other things to worry about.

The rest of the lads had now taken what cover they could, but none of it was much good. They were being fired upon from almost every angle.

Biggs shot a message down his PRR to Pearce at the rear. 'We need to move out, Pearce! You're on point. Shift it!'

Liam heard a yell and turned to his left to see a man racing towards them, his rifle slung low. This time, though, it was a SCAR, and even badly aimed it had a better chance of smashing the life out of someone than a knackered AK47.

'Cordner!' Liam yelled. 'Ten o'clock!'

In one smooth motion, Cordner was round on the attacker and sent him off his feet. Another followed and Cordner dropped him too.

'Where the feck are they all coming from?' he shouted, quickly slamming in a fresh magazine.

Liam didn't answer – he was looking at Carter, who was now lying on the ground next to him. He didn't look good: his face was pale, and blood was seeping from a wound in his belly. Another wound to his face, probably from where he'd fallen after being hit, was leaking dark blood into his red hair.

Liam called to Biggs to cover him and quickly ripped open one of the pouches in his webbing, pulling out his medical kit. With pressure on the wound, he quickly applied a field dressing. It wouldn't do much good, but at least it would stem the flow of blood.

'We have to get him out of here!' Liam yelled to Biggs. 'No way can any of us sort him out with this shit flying all around!'

Biggs yelled down the PRR again. 'Pearce! I said fucking move it, you twat! We're going to get ripped to shreds if we don't get out of here!' He then looked to Liam. 'Bollocks to this,' he said. 'Let's shift it!'

Again, Liam had Carter by one arm, while Biggs took the other, and they were legging it down the line. Cordner dropped in behind them, followed by Waterman and the others. Then Carter was snatched out of Liam's grip as Biggs caught his foot and went down hard.

Time slowed.

Liam reached for his SA80, pulled it up, made ready to give hell to whoever was about to come at them. Sound was muffled and a ringing in his ears, probably caused by the racket of rifle fire, grew louder as inexplicably the attack stilled and the world fell silent. He glanced around at the rest of the section. They were all breathing heavily, living right at the edge where life can end in a moment.

A shout barked out from somewhere to Liam's left. He stared in the direction. He couldn't see anyone who owned the voice, or make out the words – but the accent was British.

The shout came again, and he heard words this time.

'You are surrounded. There is no escape. Lay down your weapons or die where you stand!'

'Fuck you!' yelled Cordner, and a few of the other lads joined in.

A shot rang out, and down the line Liam heard a yell as Bale crumpled to the ground, blood seeping from a leg wound.

'This is your last warning,' the voice called. 'Lay down your weapons!'

Liam couldn't believe this was happening. Panic was squeezing his heart. He wanted to puke and scream and run all at once. Then he saw Biggs turn to stare at him. And the look in his eye was enough to tell him that none of them had any choice.

They were about to surrender to Al Shabaab.

14

Liam spat blood.

Having surrendered, they were now weaponless and surrounded. The thump to his face from the butt of the terrorist's AK47 would've smashed his jaw if he hadn't turned at just the right moment. Instead of crashing into his teeth at full power, it had glanced off his cheek and across his mouth, splitting his lips and bloodying his nose.

The pain of it coursed through him as he shook his head, working with every ounce of his strength to keep a lid on his fear and remember his training. The instructional video they had all watched, *Conduct Under Capture*, seemed like a distant memory. What had the bloke said? Something about accepting that you were going to get hurt, that bones would be broken, that you were going to be beaten up and there was nothing you could do about that? At the time, it had made sense that there was no point trying to prevent injury; it was more important to focus on keeping your mind secure. But now, with every possibility of facing torture, Liam really had no idea if he would be able to take it or not.

Yeah, he'd survived the training, but he hadn't been smashed in the face by a rifle during that, had he? No amount of practice role-plays could fully prepare anyone for the real thing. But it was all he had, and it had to be enough.

'*Get down!*'

The terrorists trained their guns on Liam's section and forced the soldiers to their knees. Liam braced his hands shoulder width apart on the ground to stop himself from falling with the force of the blow. In front of him he could make out the feet and legs of the terrorist who had smashed his face, laughing as he'd done it. A volatile mix of rage and terror burned inside Liam. All he wanted to do was crack the bastard in the bollocks, then rip his face off. But that wasn't an option. Not yet anyway.

The terrorist edged forward, lifted a foot and pushed Liam over onto his side. As he rolled, the man came in hard with a kick to his gut. Liam had just enough time to roll into a ball and protect himself as best he could, and somehow he managed to deflect the terrorist's foot with his knees.

A shock of pain raced through his leg and along his spine, but as Liam looked up he saw pain in the terrorist's eyes as well. The man had been expecting his toes to connect with soft flesh, but instead they'd hammered into bone and the shock of it was etched across his face. He was clearly trying to man it out, but Liam saw tears, and as the terrorist walked over to some of the other Al Shabaab gunmen milling around, he was showing a definite limp. Liam smiled to himself and hoped that the fucker had broken a toe.

Rolling himself back up onto his knees, he kept his head down. The last thing he wanted to do was aggravate the captors. It was time to be compliant, do as he was told, even though every molecule in his body was crying out to run.

The decision to surrender had, Liam knew, been made for them. It was either that or get completely over-run by the terrorists and mown down for nothing. They wouldn't have stood a chance. But that didn't make it any easier to swallow. A big part of him was already thinking that being dead would've been better than this – at least then they wouldn't have to experience the terror of anticipation. But thinking like that was no help at all. He had to remain switched on, find a way for them to escape, or hang onto the hope that they'd all be rescued.

From where he was positioned, Liam could make out the rest of his section. None of them were exactly in the best of spirits, with the terrorists strolling around, poking them with the barrels of their weapons, laughing, kicking, punching, dragging their bergens off them and throwing them to the side with the captured weaponry. Bale's injury had thankfully been only a graze – enough to knock him off his feet, but not enough to cripple him completely. He was bleeding but wasn't in a bad way, despite the agony etched across his face.

It was Carter that Liam was most concerned about. The terrorists had dragged him over to where they had moved the rest of the section for a bit of gloating and humiliation. He was still unconscious and the dressing Liam had placed on the wound was already soaked through with blood.

Amid all the chaos and confusion and fear, there was one individual all of the section had their eyes on.

The English voice that had called for them to surrender belonged to none other than Abdul Azeez. The Al Shabaab poster boy was out here with them and it was clear that he was more than a little pleased with his prize. He was strolling around like a newly crowned king, his subjects cheering his every movement, clapping and waving their arms in adoration. Liam thought back to what he'd witnessed during the CTR. Azeez was a cold-blooded bastard, and killing was something he did with as much ease as breathing. Their situation couldn't have been much worse.

Liam knew that back at the FOB, and no doubt in the UK too, word of their capture would be spreading. It wouldn't be in the news, not yet anyway – not until the terrorists decided to go global and boast about their trophies. But across the MOD, anyone who was anyone would be informed, specialists would be called up, and every avenue to secure a possible rescue would be explored. Hell, for all he knew, the SAS were probably already en route.

A foot shoved Liam in the back and he toppled forwards.

'Move!' came a gruff voice from behind him, one of the terrorist's thick Somali accent making the English word barely understandable.

Liam shuffled forwards as the foot pushed again. Around him he saw that the rest of the section was also being moved. They were being herded together like sheep – only rather than dogs doing the work, these were wolves hungry for blood. And any thought of escape was hopeless, at least for the moment. The clearing in which they'd found the KDF soldier was little more than a hundred metres away, and beyond that was a long trek through trees to the extraction point.

A minute or two later, Liam was up close with the rest of the lads. He exchanged glances with Cordner, then Biggs. No words were spoken, but the grim determination they shared in that moment was enough. They had to get through this.

Two terrorists walked over to where Carter had been dragged. They shouted to Abdul Azeez and trained their weapons down on his chest.

Oh, fuck, no . . .

Was there going to be a repeat of what he'd witnessed during the CTR? A ripple of fear coursed through Liam and the soldiers around him. He almost choked on it and desperation made him scream.

'Don't you fucking dare!' he yelled, and he wasn't alone. They weren't all just thinking and fearing the same, they were voicing it.

'Leave him be, you bastard!'

'Don't fucking touch him!'

Liam saw Abdul Azeez start to smile. He was enjoying this! Fury burned hot inside Liam and he made to move, but a rifle barrel jabbed him hard.

Then bullets rang out and everyone fell silent.

15

For a horrifying moment, Liam thought Carter had been shot, but then he spotted Abdul Azeez pointing his weapon over their heads.

'*Get down!*' The terrorist leader pulled the trigger again, just to make sure everyone got the message.

Liam realized that there was nothing any of them could do, especially without their weapons. With the terrorists fired up by their victory, he had no doubt that any attempt to fight back would potentially end with them all in trouble. Life was cheap here.

Happy that everyone was now silent and on the ground, Azeez walked over to where Carter was lying. Holding his breath, Liam waited for what seemed like the inevitable. Azeez crouched down at Carter's side and, for a moment, seemed to consider the soldier's fate. He then stood up and walked over to where Liam and the others were surrounded by the rest of the terrorists.

'The man is badly injured. I do not know if he will live. I can of course hurry him along the road to hell and kill him here and let him rot. But I am not the monster your government would have you believe. So, you can tend to him and carry him yourselves. You have five minutes.'

Liam was struck by how out of place Abdul Azeez's accent seemed in the setting. He knew there were plenty of British lads keen to carry out jihad in hotspots across the globe, but it still jarred. Azeez was eloquent too, speaking not just with clarity, but with an intelligence that made him even more dangerous. And as for not being a monster, they all knew that was a lie. Even a shark looks like it is smiling, thought Liam.

'Well?' said Abdul Azeez. 'Do none of you want to save the life of your friend?' He gave a lazy grin, and twisted his beard between his fingers. Up close, Liam noticed blood splatters on his white tunic.

Liam pushed himself to his feet.

'Go,' said Azeez. 'You now have four minutes.'

Liam raced over to Carter. His airway was clear, and he was still breathing. Pulse was weak, but it was there. Liam checked him again, top to toe, for any signs of other wounds, running through the checklist for assessing an injury. He could feel no broken bones, and the bullet was still lodged inside him somewhere as he found no exit wound. It was still just the wound to his stomach, and the dressing was soaked through. He pulled it away carefully, then poured water from his bottle over the wound. Next he removed a sachet of chemical hemostats from the medical kit in his webbing, ripped it open with his teeth, and, opening the wound with his fingers, poured the powder into it, before covering it again with a fresh dressing and applying pressure. The hemostats would help stem the bleed. That was all he could do for now.

Wiping his bloodied hands on his legs, Liam looked over to the rest of the section. They were all thinking the same thing: unless Carter got proper medical help, the soldier's chances of survival were poor to non-existent.

'You are finished?' Abdul Azeez was at Liam's side and staring down at him and Carter.

'Yes,' said Liam. 'But he needs medical attention. A doctor, a surgeon. There's only so much any of us can do.'

'Can you carry him?'

Liam nodded, though he knew that moving Carter would only make his condition worse.

'Good,' said Azeez. 'Then we shall get moving. Up!'

The final word was a barked order to the whole section. To hurry them along, the terrorists were in amongst them, kicking and punching them to their feet.

Liam waited for someone to come and help him with Carter, but when it was clear that Azeez meant for him to carry him alone, he carefully hoisted him onto his back, across his shoulders. As he walked over to where the others were now standing, Azeez signalled for his men to fetch the bergens, making the prisoners carry them again while two – as neither Liam nor Carter could carry one – were pushed towards two of his own men. It was clear that they didn't want to leave anything behind, no doubt happy to put to their own use any kit they happened to chance upon. Liam hoped they'd try the rations and choke on them.

The march to wherever they were heading began as it meant to go on, with the terrorists pushing and yelling at Liam and the others to keep moving. The ground was flat, though their progress was hidden from prying eyes by trees and brush. With Carter's weight on him, Liam soon began to fatigue, but he refused to give in. The pain in his back matched that in his legs and feet and each step was an effort. Yet he kept going, pushing the pain deep down and locking it away. For all he knew, if he stopped the terrorists might simply shoot him on the spot and keep on moving. After a while, though, as daylight ebbed and darkness slipped across the land, Liam began to falter. Then his foot twisted and he stumbled, dropping to his knees and falling forward with Carter toppling over his head. Shouts came at him immediately, then a kick into the ribs, but he couldn't move. He needed water, he needed rest. He wasn't about to be given either.

'Up! Up! Move!'

The terrorist yelling at him had death in his eyes and his finger was on the trigger. Liam struggled to his feet, reached down for Carter, but it was too much. There was no way he could carry him any further.

'*Move!*'

Liam was exhausted, couldn't move, had nothing left. Then Pearce and Cordner were next to him, lifting him up and grabbing Carter, even as punches and kicks rained down on them both.

A shove in his back and Liam was moving again. With Carter off his shoulders and only a bergen to carry, it initially felt like he was weightless, but then the tiredness and fear kicked back in and reminded him that he was anything but. All he could do now was focus on putting one foot in front of the other and just keeping moving.

When darkness took over completely, the sky above bright with moonlight and stars, they were allowed a break, but for only a few minutes. Water was passed round, as were more slaps and yells.

For the rest of the trek they all took it in turns to carry Carter. All except Bale, who was struggling along with his bleeding leg.

Despite everything that was happening, Liam still managed to stay alert enough to keep a track of their direction. OK, so their destination was unknown, but if he was able to keep some idea in his head of where they were heading, and where they had come from, he might have a chance of navigating his way back should he ever break free. The stars were all he had, but it was enough, and he kept glancing up, forcing himself to memorize not just their position but the direction in which they were heading.

Just when it seemed like the march would never end, he and the others were pushed and jabbed into a clearing, which was covered by a thick canopy of trees above. It struck Liam that the only way to find a location like this would be to know where to look in the first place. It was well hidden from prying eyes.

A narrow track, carved out in the main by tyres, led off from the clearing, and around it sat a number of structures. Liam counted six, all built from staves cut from the surrounding trees, with corrugated iron roofs. It was into these that Liam and the rest of the section were shoved with little care and a not inconsiderable amount of glee, once their kit had been removed.

Inside, the soldiers had their first chance to speak to one another. Not that there was much to say, or that could be said.

In the corner of the shack, Liam found Waterman and Biggs, with Carter lying on the ground. The floor was dirt and there was no matting to rest on or keep away the cold that was seeping up from the earth to chill them all.

'How is he?'

'God knows how he's still alive,' said Waterman. 'Must be a stubborn bastard, that's all I can say.'

Liam knelt down beside them. Carter was barely breathing. His face was pale and clammy with sweat, and his eyes were sunk deep into his skull. Liam looked up at Biggs. 'Is there nothing more we can do?'

'Make sure he's comfortable, and that's about it,' said Biggs. 'Those bastards have our medical supplies now, so I can't even clean the wound again.' There was anger and compassion in Biggs's voice. He wanted to do something, but was wholly helpless. They all were.

Liam leaned against the side of the shack. Around him the rest of the lads did the same. Eight men, including Carter, utterly exhausted. Whatever hell they were now in, he knew beyond doubt that it was going to get a whole lot worse.

Closing his eyes, he talked himself out of giving in to

fear. It was a struggle. This was the most terrifying position he'd been in his entire life. If he thought about all the things that could possibly happen, he knew he'd go mad and be of no use to anyone.

He had to hold it together: they all did . . .

Liam was woken by a kick in his side, but was more shocked by the fact that exhaustion had taken over and made him fall asleep. As he struggled to rouse himself, he was dragged up and out of the shack. The same was happening to them all. Once outside, they were led off individually into the surrounding trees by Al Shabaab men.

Only one thought was in Liam's mind now: he was about to be executed. Why else would this be happening? What other reason could there be?

He thought fast. He had to make a break for it. There was no other option. Perhaps, if he overpowered the two men with him, he would have a chance? He could take one, of that he was confident, but he would have to be quick to take them both, and luck would need to play its part. Then if he was successful, he would be armed. Heading back, he could take out the other terrorists, release his friends—

'Stop!'

The voice hooked Liam away from his thoughts.

What had they stopped him for? Was this it? Was he about to get slotted? He had to act now. This was his last chance!

The butt of an AK47 crashed into his back. As the pain burst through him, another strike buckled his legs. Before he could react and stop himself from tumbling, a boot was in his back, hoofing him forward.

Liam fell, air rushing past as darkness swallowed him. He made a blind grab for anything, but there was nothing solid until he landed hard, face first, mouth filling with muck and grit. He forced himself up onto his knees, winded. Initially he thought the fall had blinded him. He could see nothing at all. Then his eyes focused and he realized he was at the bottom of a deep hole. He looked up, expecting to see his two guards readying their rifles for the *coup de grâce*. But instead they were laughing and waving.

'What the fuck is going on?' Liam shouted.

'Have a nice stay!' said one of the men, then they both waved as they dropped a makeshift wooden cage door over the top of the hole and walked off.

Liam stood up to get some bearings on his new prison. Pain coursed through him; his joints were stiff and every bit of him was sore. The hole, he guessed, was at least three metres deep. He tried to jump and grab onto the cage door, but all his fingers did was glance off it before he fell back down. He checked the walls, looking for some way of climbing out, but the sides were slick with grime and utterly impossible to scale. He jumped again and touched the door blocking his exit, but it didn't budge; it was clearly weighed down. The bottom of the hole was about one and a half metres square. Liam tried to lie diagonally across it, but his legs were still bent.

Had they left him here to die? Why hadn't they just shot him and got it over and done with?

16

'What the—'

A stone hit his skull with a stinging thump. Liam immediately covered himself with his arms and crawled as tightly as he could into a corner of the hole. Were they going to stone him now? Then something fell into the hole. It was a rope ladder. Liam glanced up to see two terrorists looking down at him, their rifles silhouetted against the early morning sun. They weren't coming down. They wanted him to climb up.

Once out of the hole, Liam was dropped to the ground and his hands tied behind his back. He struggled but soon gave up. There was no point wasting energy. Then he was lifted up and marched forwards, before a kidney punch dropped him and he found himself sprawled in front of Abdul Azeez and his men.

A hand slapped him across the left side of his head so hard that he was sure his eardrum had burst. Barely conscious, his whole body exhausted from the ordeal of the last twenty-four hours, Liam was hardly able to compute what the hell was going on. The hole didn't make sense, and neither did being dragged out of it. For a moment he'd half believed it was a nightmare, that he was trapped in a dream. Even as the ropes had been tied round his wrists, his arms trapped behind him, he had shaken his head in an attempt to wake himself up. Then the blurry image of a man he knew appeared in front of him, the slap had come, and with stars shattering his vision, reality had crashed into Liam with the force of a shotgun fired at point blank.

'I would like you to tell me who you are and why you are here.'

Liam raised his head to find Azeez smiling back at him. He had the kind of face that in any other circumstances Liam would have trusted, but his hard eyes revealed just what he was capable of.

'Scott, Liam, Lance—' he began, remembering his interrogation training.

Another slap came in hard from the other side and Liam, unable to stop himself toppling over, crashed onto his side, knocking his shoulder. Rough hands grabbed him, had him upright again.

'That is for looking into my eyes,' said Azeez. 'I have killed people for showing such disrespect.'

189

Liam lowered his gaze.

'Now, again,' said Azeez. 'Who are you, why are you here?'

Liam took a breath, gave his name, rank and number, but nothing else. He readied himself for another blow. That was one thing he did remember from the video about being captured. Your captors wanted to hurt you and that was what they were going to do. But it was your mind that you had to hold onto, that more than anything else.

'None of you are carrying personal items,' said Azeez. 'You have no wallets, no photographs, no identification documents or tags. This tells me that you are Special Forces.'

Liam said nothing. Being in Recce Platoon carried certain risks, and capture was – as he now knew for sure – one of them. For that reason, any soldier carrying out such a role had to leave their ID behind.

'So, your silence speaks volumes,' said Azeez with a fox's smile. 'You are SAS, I think. The best of the best. Who dares wins, yes?' He laughed. It was a chilling sound, like a hyena drunk on blood. 'It seems that you dared, but that you did not win, my friend.'

I'm not your friend, thought Liam.

'So, if you are SAS, then what was your mission?'

Liam kept his eyes low and repeated his name – as

much to hear his own voice as anything.

'Shall *I* tell *you*?' said Azeez, leaning in towards Liam. 'Yes, I think I shall. It was to capture me, I think. That's why you were sent in with the KDF. But as you're now aware, we knew of that mission long ago. And we were glorious in our victory! They were given into our hands like lambs for the sacrifice. It was a blessing.'

A blessing? thought Liam. How could someone think that the killing of other human beings was a blessing? Behind him, he heard cheers from the Al Shabaab henchmen.

'And now,' continued Azeez, moving to address his men, 'we have the additional prize of Her Majesty's SAS!'

More cheering, but Liam wasn't listening. He found it almost amusing that Azeez assumed they were the SAS. It showed just how important he figured himself to be for the British to send the Special Forces in to snatch him.

Azeez moved closer to Liam. It was a deliberately slow movement, a man of self-assured importance, royalty almost, making sure his every move was noticed by his followers.

'You belong to me now,' he said. 'Not to your queen. Not to your government. No one will come for you. No one will find you. And soon, but not quite yet, you will die. It is, I am afraid, a certainty. There is nothing you or anyone else can do about it. Are you prepared for death?'

Liam didn't answer.

'Your silence will also be broken, my friend,' said Azeez. 'As easily as a butterfly's wing.'

And with that, Liam was grabbed by his arms and dragged over to his hole, where his hands were cut free and he was kicked down into the darkness again.

Back in the hole, Liam tried to gather his thoughts. He traced the direction he'd followed with the stars and figured they'd ended up some ten kilometres south-east of where they had surrendered. That was something, and offered a glimmer of hope – but only if he was able to escape. And that was looking impossible. But he was still alive, though living in a hole wasn't going to help. It offered no protection, no warmth, no comfort. A grave, waiting for him to give up and die. He wasn't about to do that, no matter how bad the odds were.

No food was offered, only water, which was brown with muck and dirt. He knew it was probably riddled with germs and parasites, but he would worry about that if and when he got out of this hell. For now, he had to stay alive. So he drank it, though the stench of it – a foul mix of rotting vegetation and something else he didn't even want to guess at – made him retch. The only way to get it down was to hold his breath until the liquid reached his stomach, and even then it took all his will power not to throw it back up.

Later, the hunger gnawing at him grew so bad that he scrabbled around looking for anything in the hole that might pass as food. All he managed to find was worms wriggling their way out of the walls. He'd eaten them before, back in basic training, but only when thrown in with other food as extra protein. They hadn't exactly been tasty then. He'd heard the best way was to dry them out and then crumble them into water. But that wasn't an option here. So he dug into the muck and pulled one out. It was fat and wriggled in his hand, twisting itself into knots to try and escape. Liam shoved it into his mouth and chewed. The wriggling and writhing continued, and when the worm burst, the acrid taste of the jelly inside was too much and he spat it out. Water would have to do.

A full day and night passed by before Liam was next dragged out to be questioned. This time Azeez observed from the sidelines, like a lion watching his pack play with fresh meat. Two of the terrorists took it in turns to slap Liam around, knock him to the ground, shout at him, spit at him, force the barrels of their rifles into his mouth. Azeez called out to them to hit him harder, laughing as Liam tried his best to protect himself from the beating.

The next interrogation came up quicker, though Liam wondered if he had simply lost track of time. He gave no more information, even though the beating was worse than ever, his right eye swelling up from a punch that made him yell. Thrown back in the hole, bruises blazed all over him and every slight movement caused him pain. The damp of the hole was slowly rotting his skin. He could now peel it off his fingers like soft dough.

He realized then that he hadn't seen or heard anyone from the section. Not counting Carter, there were six other men out there who were probably going through the same ordeal as him. At least, he hoped they were – the only other option was that they'd been shot, but he refused to think about that. If he was being kept alive, for whatever purpose, then surely the others were too. He held onto the thought that Azeez valued them all as prisoners and so would keep them alive, though perhaps not necessarily in one piece.

Knowing the only way to survive was to keep his mind intact, Liam focused on all the things that made him who he was now, the person he had become. Life before the army was so distant that the images he had of it were tattered and faded and seemed to belong to another person. The army had forced him to change, to become something so startlingly different to what he had ever believed possible that the more he thought about it, the more astonished he became by his own progress and development.

He was no longer the kid who hated school, wasted his time free running around derelict warehouses with a few mates, and couldn't wait to leave home. A kid who had watched his best mate fall to his death when one stunt had gone terribly wrong. It had been a turning point in his life, one that had put him on the road to joining the army. Now he had a proper life, friends, skills, and a duty not just to himself, but to those he served with.

Liam remembered the first stages of his training back in Harrogate, the shock of the regime, the fitness, the relentless barrage of information. He forced himself to revive old things he had forgotten, sifting through his brain for any pieces of information that would help him survive what he was experiencing now. He ran through the escape and evasion training, playing it out like a movie in his mind. He rehearsed his star navigation, concealment skills, hand-to-hand combat. He wondered where it would lead him if – no, *when* – he got out. His brief time in the army had already given him so much adventure, so many experiences.

He wasn't ready to quit.

* * *

It was dark again when, having been dragged from his hole for the nth time, everything changed for Liam. Exhausted and stiff, battered and bruised, bleeding and so hungry he wanted to scream, he was once more forced to the ground in front of Abdul Azeez. Liam knew he had nothing more to say. He'd stuck with his training, given only his name, rank and number even as the beatings had grown more severe. And with each one he had survived, it was a small victory. They had broken his body but not his will.

'We meet again, Liam,' said Azeez.

Liam kept his eyes to the ground, readied himself for the inevitable kicks and punches that would leave him dazed and bleeding. What was another bruise?

'We are like old friends now, I think,' said Azeez.

Liam kept his mouth shut.

'Now,' said Azeez, 'I have decided two things.' His voice was calm, almost kind in its delivery, as though he were talking to someone he truly cared for. 'One: I need to know from you where the rest of your men are placed, the rest of the KDF. I know that they are not at the main base you soldiers use like some holiday camp in Kenya. No, they are closer, or else they would not have been able to attack as they did.'

Liam would never give away that location. Not a

chance. Nothing could make him betray the others.

'The second thing I have decided is this . . .' Azeez paused then, and Liam, his blood running cold, saw him close up as he leaned in to whisper in his ear, 'I think we have been going about this all wrong, Liam. That is what I think. And I've come up with a new approach to see if I can make you talk. It's a good idea, yes?'

Christ, thought Liam, the fucker sounds almost pleased with himself. He wondered just what else they could do, what other possible tortures they had in mind.

A dragging sound from his left caught Liam's attention. Risking a look, he saw two of Azeez's men hauling a soldier towards them. It was Carter. And he was still alive.

'Your friend here,' said Azeez, 'is strong, it seems. I don't know how he hasn't yet died. But as you can see for yourself, he is conscious. Who knows – perhaps he could make it through another few days, maybe longer?'

Liam went cold. What did Azeez want with Carter? Why had they dragged him out here?

Carter was dropped just about a metre from where Liam was kneeling in the mud. He looked terrible, but his eyes were open and he was staring up at Liam. His lips moved, muttered something, but Liam couldn't hear it, couldn't understand. In an attempt to comfort him,

Liam forced a smile, but he knew it was a hollow gesture.

'Now,' said Azeez, 'I am going to give you something, Liam. That's the kind of person I am. Generous! Yes, I am going to give you the most precious thing in the world!'

Whatever it was, Liam didn't want it. He carried on staring at Carter, whose eyes were glassy and unfocused. Hang on, he thought, silently willing his mate to cling onto life, to not give in. *Hang on . . .*

'A life!' said Azeez. 'That is my gift to you, Liam. The life of your friend here. It's yours! What a great and wondrous gift, yes?'

A sickness took root in Liam's stomach. It grew and grew, twisting through his body, making him dizzy.

'You see,' said Azeez. 'Now that you have your friend's life, it is yours to do with as you will! You can throw it away, or you can save it! Such power does not come to all men, my friend. So, you are truly blessed at this moment.'

The sickness turned into cold barbs of steel, piercing Liam with the agony of what was unfolding.

'So, will you save it, Liam? That's the question, is it not? Will you save your friend if I give you that chance? For I am willing to do that right now! All you have to do is tell me where the rest of your soldiers are. See?

It's simple! Just answer my question truthfully, and he lives. For how long I cannot say, but you will have given him that extra time, and in exchange for so small a thing.'

Helpless, Liam watched as Azeez stood up and walked over to Carter, kneeling down beside him. With a tenderness that struck Liam as disturbing, he then reached out and ever so gently rested Carter's head in his lap, stroking his pale, damp forehead.

'His life is in your hands now, Liam,' said the Al Shabaab leader, and placed a pistol on the ground at his side. It was a Glock, one clearly stolen from the section. 'Will you save it? Or will you throw it away?'

The reality of what he was offering crashed into Liam and he screamed, but his throat, so dry and sore, barely emitted a note. He remembered what had happened during his training, but this time it was for real, and he knew full well that Azeez wasn't just playing games.

'Tell me, Liam. Tell me what I want to know, and you will save your friend. *Tell me.*'

'I can't,' Liam eventually managed.

'You know, I think you can . . .' Azeez reached for his pistol and pulled back the cocking slide.

'No, you're not listening,' said Liam. 'I don't *know* the location. Not exactly . . .'

And it was the truth. He had a rough idea, but that

was all. He'd been more focused on the job than anything else.

Azeez placed the pistol close to Carter's head. 'This is
my gift to you, Liam,' he said, voice silky smooth and
honey sweet. 'The life of your friend!'

Liam, tears in his eyes, torn apart by panic and fear,
glanced down at Carter. He could do nothing, say
nothing. He was helpless.

'Liam?'

Liam caught Carter's eyes, mouthed, 'I'm sorry . . .'

Azeez pulled the trigger.

17

'Liam!'

The voice was one he recognized, one that sounded exhausted but relieved to see him. Liam raised his head, though it pained him to do so, his whole neck seemingly now made of nothing but bruises.

'Pearce?'

'Too fucking right it is,' Pearce replied, his voice dry and hacking.

Liam couldn't speak, had no words. After seeing Carter murdered right in front of him, he had been beaten again before being dragged not back to his hole this time – which was some relief – but to the shack he and the rest of the section had first been placed in. The rest of the lads were there too. And from what he could see in the moonlight, they all looked in a shit state.

'Carter . . .' Liam managed. 'I—'

'We heard the shot,' said another voice. It was Biggs.

And for such a big man, in both size and personality, he seemed shrunk somehow. But the fight still remained in his eyes, diamond hard.

'Azeez . . . he shot Carter,' Liam explained, fighting tears and failing badly. 'I couldn't do anything to save him. I couldn't!'

'I know,' said Biggs. 'I know.'

And then Liam finally gave in to it. The torment of the days and nights they'd been captive, the beatings and the hunger, the empty hopelessness of it all, the terror of not knowing if the next interrogation would be his last and, finally, the brutal murder of Carter. He sobbed and the tears flowed freely, tracing white lines down his soiled face.

'Let him be,' said Biggs to the others around him, and Liam felt a firm hand on his back.

When there were no more tears to cry, and Liam had at last crawled out of the black sorrow that had so quickly overwhelmed him, he sat up and took in the state of the other soldiers. Black eyes rode proud on faces cut and bleeding. But not one of them yet looked ready to give in. Indeed, now that they were all back together again, they seemed almost fired up by it, ready to keep fighting.

As Waterman explained, they had all been separated. 'Like you,' he said, 'we all got taken off, thrown into a hole. The beatings and the questioning, we all had it.'

'They put us on our own to try and break us,' said Liam.

'Exactly,' said Biggs. 'And it didn't work. You were the last to return. I think Azeez had just had enough, which is why he did what he did to Carter.'

'I want to kill that bastard,' said Liam.

'If there was a queue, then you probably jumped to the front, mate,' said Pearce, leaning in. 'What he did to Carter, and that he made you watch it? Death's too good for him, but it's what he fucking well deserves. And a slow one.'

Cordner crawled over.

'How's life?' Liam asked.

'I'm gaspin' for a draw,' said Cordner. 'I'd smoke cow shit wrapped in bog roll right now.'

'That's a lovely thought,' said Liam.

'Wouldn't make his breath smell any worse, though,' said Pearce.

The sound of friendly voices, and the immediate soldier banter, lit something within Liam that brought him back on line. There was still hope here, he realized. And he needed that now more than ever.

'So what now?' he asked.

'Well, I'm not sure we've time to dig a tunnel,' said Pearce.

'I overheard Azeez talking about something when I was being dragged out of the hole, this one time,' Cordner commented. 'He mentioned a negotiator.'

'What do you mean?' Liam asked.

'While we're out here in the shit,' Cordner continued, 'back home all hell will have broken loose. All channels of communication will have been explored and I'm guessing they've managed to find one and open it enough to get Azeez to speak to a negotiator.'

This news was like a shot of espresso to Liam's weary mind. 'You mean they're trying to get us released?'

'I can't see anyone in the MOD getting any sleep at the minute,' said Cordner. 'This kind of stuff, well, it's bad for business, isn't it?'

'But Azeez's not going to let us just walk out of this, is he?' said Liam. 'He's not an idiot. This is probably the best thing that's ever happened to him!'

'True,' said Pearce. 'But a negotiator is just a small part in a big engine. Who knows what the fuck is going on behind the scenes?'

'It's probably buying us time, and that's a plus,' said Airey. 'The longer we are alive, the better chance we have of something happening that'll give us the opportunity to turn this around.'

Considering their circumstances, Liam was impressed

to hear his mates being so positive. 'You saying we have an escape plan?' he asked.

Biggs shook his head. 'No, not yet. We've all been separated, and that's probably another reason why – they didn't want us ganging up and breaking out.'

'So why are we back together now?'

As if in response, the shack door was kicked flying and a group of gunmen came charging in, yelling and jabbing everyone with the barrels of their AK47s.

Liam was on his feet and herded outside with the others. His first thought was that this was it; they were being led outside to be mown down by Azeez and his shiny new SCAR. But then he saw the truck in front of them.

Liam had no idea what make it was, though judging by the numerous random body panels and odd wheels, it would be impossible to trace it to an original. It was a large flatbed truck, probably a seven and a half tonner, with a canvas hood, and had probably spent its life being used to carry everything from farm equipment and animals to furniture and Al Shabaab militants. Now it was going to transport a group of knackered, beaten soldiers from the British Army to God knew where.

More shouts came from the terrorists, and Liam and the others were quickly pushed into the back of the truck. Inside, the floor was in places non-existent and the ground below them was clearly visible. Once they were all in, their equipment was thrown after them, though noticeably without their weapons.

'Well, at least they're sensible enough to know to hang onto quality kit when they see it,' said Pearce. 'Though I'm not best pleased about the idea of some Al Shabaab twat bedding down some time soon in my doss bag.'

'Mate, that's a bonus! Your doss bag's a fecking biological weapon!' Cordner joked.

The truck shuddered as the engine wheezed into life with a sound like the undead breaking free from the grave. Then it moved, jostling Liam and the others around with all the care of a rattle in the hand of a griping baby.

Moving off, Liam stared out of the back of the truck. Something caught his eye in the darkness. A shadow, lying on the ground, still and lifeless. It was Carter's body, left for the wildlife.

The truck moved at a snail's pace, hampered by a rough track, darkness and an engine that wanted to give up every time the tyres struggled. The thrum and rumble of movement was hypnotizing and Liam fought against sleep. He had passed the stage of exhaustion and a strange force inside him was keeping him awake. So again he traced their direction, making a mental note of the geography of where they were driving through, any features that stood out that would help him find his way back, should he ever get the chance to make a break.

When the journey eventually came to an end, Liam reckoned they had travelled only a few miles, but it had taken what seemed like for ever. It was still dark, but dawn was creeping its way across the Somali landscape.

With the truck stationary, the rear was dropped open, the harsh clang of it swinging down echoing painfully in Liam's ears.

'Out!' The barked order was accompanied by hands reaching inside to haul the soldiers from the truck.

They tumbled like coal tipped out of a sack, falling into each other as their legs struggled to stop them crumpling to the ground, numb from the journey and unresponsive.

A clatter of rifle fire sprayed overhead. Liam looked up to see Abdul Azeez standing in front of them. His clothes were now smeared with Carter's blood and his calm demeanour added to the coldness which seeped from him. Behind, hidden in the greying darkness, was what at first glance looked like a derelict farmstead. There were a number of brick buildings, all with tin roofs.

Liam switched himself on, eyeing everything around

him. He counted five buildings, all of them tucked in close around a central area of dirt about the size of a small car park. Beyond the perimeter of the buildings was thick brush and rocky outcrops, a clump of trees concealing the farmstead from prying eyes. A sense of dread crept up to Liam and twisted his gut. He had no doubt that, as far as Abdul Azeez was concerned, this was the end of the road for his prisoners.

'This,' said Azeez, 'is your new home.'

The man laughed then, and Liam hated him even more. A rifle barrel jabbed him in the side, forcing him to move. Herded like sheep, he and the others were marched towards the buildings.

'I knew it was worth complaining to the management,' said Pearce. 'See? They've upgraded us. Result.'

Liam was about to reply when out of nowhere a rifle butt swung in and caught Pearce square across the side of his face. The force of it knocked his head round to the right and he stumbled, but managed to stop himself dropping to his knees. When Pearce stood up again, Liam saw that the blow had opened up a gash down his cheek. He also saw the soldier clench his fists and stare at the man who had hit him. They were all at a point now where it would take little to make them snap. He hoped to God that his mate could hold it together and not retaliate.

'No talking!' yelled the gunman. 'No talking or you will die!'

Liam saw Pearce take a step towards him, but Biggs reached out and rested a hand on his arm, shaking his head.

Pearce held back, but only just.

'Walk!'

Bloodied but unbowed, they moved on towards the buildings. Once they were inside, Liam could see that the farmstead had been filled with cages, each just large enough to allow a man room to stand in a crouch and to lie down. The cages were dirty, rusted things, the floors covered in greasy, muck-stained sacking and cloth. But almost worse than that was the smell. It was a stink of human waste and sweat, of people left to rot, and it stung his eyes. The taste of it in his mouth made him heave, but with nothing to chuck up all he did was cough, his stomach bucking hard and painful.

'You're fucking kidding me,' said Biggs. 'We're not dogs.'

One of the gunmen grabbed him and pushed him into the first cage, locking it shut behind him. Then one by one the others were locked into their own cages.

Liam waited his turn. He had to be compliant now, but keep an eye out for an opportunity. And when it

of resistance to Al Shabaab. My life is in your hands. This demand must be met within seven days.'

With the words spoken, the video was paused, and Abdul Azeez gave a nod. Liam was lifted off the floor.

'You're a natural, Scott,' said Azeez, as Liam was taken back through the door. 'The camera loves you. The world will see you through it. You will be famous!'

Liam held his stare, but stayed quiet.

'You do not fear me, I see. That's good. I admire it. But it will serve you no purpose, I assure you.'

Liam imagined himself leaping forward on top of Azeez, driving him into the wall behind him, hammering his head up into the man's chin to break his face, then tearing into him to rip his life to shreds.

'You are meant to die, you see?' Azeez continued. 'We do not expect our demands to be met, but we do expect the world to shudder at our acts. It will learn eventually to leave us alone. Sometimes, brutality serves a purpose.'

Liam was then marched to his cage, the door shut behind him as he stumbled forwards. He turned to see Pearce led out for his own moment of fame. Liam thought about what he had just said, the lies that no one would believe and the deadline that would never be adhered to. The British government never gave in to terrorist demands. Period.

Even if Al Shabaab's calls *were* met, he didn't trust

Azeez one bit. And that meant that once those seven days were up, he and the rest of the section, and the KDF lads too, were dead.

Liam knew that they were going to have to get themselves out of the shit. He also knew that when he next got into that room with the camera, he wouldn't be leaving it.

18

The cage stank. Every time he moved, the rags beneath him would release a new blast of the foul reek into the air, filling his nostrils with a stomach-churning aroma of vomit, sweat and excrement. Liam breathed through his mouth to limit the awfulness of it, but the smell was so thick he could taste it in the back of his throat and it clung there, infecting him inside and out.

The cages, though next to each other, were all separated by thin sheets of corrugated metal, adding to the isolation that Liam felt. He could hear the others shuffling around, breathing, but that was it. With a guard constantly patrolling, speaking to each other was impossible. And the guard made sure of this by occasionally jabbing a rifle barrel into the cage or spitting insults.

In an attempt to stop himself seizing up completely he tried to do regular stretching exercises, but it wasn't easy. His body was racked with pain and he couldn't stand fully upright in the tiny cage.

With no windows, Liam had no idea if it was day or night. The room itself was never in complete darkness – a bare bulb hung from the ceiling on a grubby length of dangerous-looking flex. The light it emitted was flickering and sparse, but it still stabbed at his tired eyes like a strobe on the blink. The guards rotated every couple of hours and used the opportunity to hurl insults at their prisoners, rattle the cages, threaten them, so any sleep that had been stolen was quickly broken.

Food came twice daily on a metal plate, along with water in a broken plastic beaker thick with dirt. Liam never gave himself time to think about what he was eating, guzzling it down before his tongue registered any taste. If he looked too closely at it he knew there was no chance it would get past his lips. But at least it was better than the worm he'd spat out back in the hole. He found himself fantasizing about army rations, pretending that each mouthful didn't taste of puke at all, but the best boil-in-the-bags in the world. In his exhausted state it was hard to keep track of time, but Liam kept a tally of meals by tearing off a small section of the rotting floor with every plate that was brought to him. Each piece of material brought them closer to the end of the seven-day deadline.

The only time Liam ever got to leave his cage was to relieve himself. He guessed that this was because none of the guards were very keen to end up with the job of mucking out the cages or dealing with prisoners covered in their own faeces. Not that it made any real difference to the smell. Leading them to the latrine was just another excuse to push their prisoners around, trip them up, punch them. None of it was ever life-threatening, but it served to keep the hostages in check. Liam knew that fighting back would only lead to a proper kicking. But he used this time to observe, always looking for a way they might be able to escape.

It was when Liam was brought his sixth meal, and thus knew by his natty use of scrap material that it was the end of his third day in the cages, that he at last spotted that hole and saw a possible chance to get the hell out.

The guards had just changed, which brought the usual barrage of insults and threats, all accompanied by the brandishing of weapons. Liam hadn't seen Abdul Azeez since his time in front of the video camera, and judging by the way the new guard was behaving, he wasn't anywhere close by. Liam knew that alcohol was a big no-no in Islam, but it was clear that this guard wasn't too fussed about that. When he spoke, his words were slurred, and when he came over with the food, there was the stench of booze on his breath, sweet and warm and sickly, like the smell of a pub the morning after.

Liam wondered just how loyal to the lofty aims of Al Shabaab the man was. More than likely he was just a gun for hire, happy to go with the highest bidder, probably because it paid better than anything else in the area and came with food, accommodation, a chance to beat someone up, and a free weapon.

Unable to communicate with the rest of the section, or indeed to check if anyone else had an escape plan in mind, Liam knew he had no choice but to just go for it – even if that meant the others were left behind. If he was able to get out and get away, and hopefully make it back to the FOB with enough intelligence about where they were imprisoned, it was the best chance any of them had of escaping.

Liam called the guard, and he stumbled over, confirming Liam's suspicions.

'What?'

'I'm sick, I think I'm going to throw up,' said Liam, forcing his voice to come out as though he was in pain and couldn't wait much longer before exploding.

'Not my problem,' said the guard, leaning against the cage.

Liam immediately decided to lay it on thick and doubled over as though in agony.

'My guts,' he moaned. 'I'm ill. Help me, please! I just need to throw up. Then I'll feel better, I know it.'

'You can die for all I care,' said the guard. 'You are worth nothing to me.'

The man's breath slipped across Liam as he leaned in close to the cage. God, thought Liam, he smelled of meths. So he screamed. But not just a yell, a raging howl that made his ears ring. Then, to add to the drama, he thrashed around in the cage, throwing himself against it as though trying to break out.

'I'm fucking dying!' he cried, retching at the same time. 'Please – help me!'

Liam knew he was risking a lot by making his act so over the top, but he had no choice – it was now or never. He had to make the guard want to get him out of that cage. And he figured that despite what he'd said, a dead prisoner would not be a good thing to have to explain to Abdul Azeez.

The guard made to leave, but as Liam continued to scream he hesitated, clearly thinking twice about what he was going to do next.

'Please,' said Liam, his voice now a broken whimper, 'please . . . help me . . .'

It wasn't difficult to fake being feeble. He felt proper grotty inside and out, and the desperation to get out was caught on every word.

The guard turned and stood in front of Liam's cage and waved his weapon threateningly. It was one of the SCARs and Liam didn't want the drunken idiot accidentally discharging it in his or anyone else's direction. The man was clearly proud of it and had even slotted a bayonet onto the end, no doubt to make it look more threatening.

'I'm begging you . . .' he moaned.

The guard moved forward and unlocked Liam's cage. 'Out!' he ordered.

Liam crawled out and stood up. The guard was immediately behind him, the end of the bayonet in his back with just enough pressure to get him shifting.

'Walk!'

Liam moved forwards, staggering down the line of cages. He tried to catch the eye of the other occupants but was out of the building before he had a chance.

The air outside was like nectar compared with what he had to breathe in his cage, and he sucked in deep gulps of it. Light was low as evening was settling in. That was good, he thought. If it had been bright daylight, his escape would be all the harder.

Again, the guard jabbed Liam, forcing him to march towards the latrine. It was nothing more than a rickety wooden frame built over a hole round the back of one of the buildings, and the stench grew stronger as they drew nearer. Liam looked around for the other guards. But there was no other movement, no sound.

The guard followed Liam round to the latrine with the barrel of his rifle up, the bayonet still scratching against Liam's back. They were alone now, out of sight of any possible onlookers. This was it. Now or never. Liam just hoped the guard was as drunk as he seemed to be.

Pulling on every ounce of energy he still had inside him, he whirled round on the guard, in one fluid motion pushing the automatic rifle out to the side with his left arm, and at the same time charging into the man's face with the fist of his right. With the momentum he now had, he punched his enemy, pummelling his face violently, splitting his nose and filling his mouth with blood from a burst lip and bitten tongue.

The guard stumbled backwards and Liam was on top of him, crushing him with his own weight as they fell to the ground, the rifle dropping from the man's grasp. At last regaining some of his senses, the man tried to punch back, but Liam gave no quarter. Fighting for his life, he found a rock with his left hand and brought it hard across the terrorist's head, knocking him silent with a single blow. The guard, stunned, reached for Liam's throat, but Liam brought the rock down again, then a third time. When he came in for a fourth blow, the guard had fallen limp beneath him.

Liam paused, rock raised and ready, but the man just lay still, blood flowing from wounds to his head. For a moment Liam thought he was simply unconscious, but checking the man's pulse told him otherwise.

Giving himself no chance to rest, he grabbed the SCAR, the few spare mags the guard had been carrying on him, and made to leg it, but realized it was probably best to at least hide the guard's body first.

He grabbed the man by the arms and dragged him along the ground to the latrine. The hole was deep, and with a shove he toppled the body over the edge and into the foul depths below. There was probably enough excrement down there to hide him for an eternity, Liam thought.

Alone now, he was faced with a choice. Head off by himself – or release the others?

19

Armed now with the SCAR, Liam felt for the first time since everything had gone to rat shit that he and the rest of the lads had a fighting chance. Maybe he could get them all out, after all. He started to make his way back to the cages.

Edging round the wall of the building, he waited a moment to see if there was any movement. He hadn't seen any of the other terrorists for a while, though he had no doubt they were in the grounds somewhere. But as the place was so quiet, all he could assume was that they were asleep. They had no reason not to be. As far as they were concerned their prisoners were under lock and key, in a shit state, and a guard was still keeping an eye on them – albeit a drunken one. Probably thought it was the easiest job in the world.

With a deep breath, Liam started forward, sticking to the shadows. The evening was really drawing in now and the grey light was fading, a deep blackness slipping in to replace it. Keeping to the wall of the latrine building, Liam huddled in tight against a door and made to dash across the gap between it and the prison building. But as he did so, the sound of an engine roared and bright lights cut across the area in front of him. The battered truck was back, and bringing with it a whole world of trouble. It was filled with more armed men and they were making their presence known, letting off shots into the air and whooping with excitement, and it wasn't just the khat that had got them buzzed, thought Liam. Something else had clearly got them wired and he didn't fancy staying around to find out what.

Unable to race back to where he'd come from, he quickly checked the door behind him, heard no sound coming from within the building, no telltale light seeping out from underneath, and slipped inside.

The rattle and clatter of the approaching truck and its occupants forced Liam to hold his breath. He had to think fast. He could hear the men jumping out of the truck now, shouting and laughing like they'd won a great battle. He didn't like the sound of it at all. Happy terrorists was a bad sign. And with that kind of movement going on, Liam knew that the missing guard was going to be discovered sooner rather than later.

Outside, the engine was killed, only to be replaced by the sound of cheering. Liam had no doubt that the ruckus was for one reason only: Abdul Azeez had clearly been away somewhere, but was now back.

Liam thought about the rest of the section and the KDF soldiers all still shut in their stinking cages. He had to get them out. It was his duty. What if they ended up being shot as punishment for his escape? Or what if he got lost and died in the attempt? The questions rammed into his mind as quick as machine-gun fire, but he had no answers, only what-ifs. If things quietened down, there was still an outside chance that he could get over there and free them. But he was just one man against a whole gang of armed thugs – what chance did he or any of them stand?

Thoughts and outcomes rained down on him and Liam forced himself to focus, think straight. But it was no good. Exhaustion, pain, fatigue, hunger, fear; they were all coming at him at once, knocking any sensible thoughts clear from his mind. He couldn't decide what to do, just couldn't. It was all too much. He leaned against the wall, sinking to the ground. But as he did so, he brushed against something. As his eyes slowly adjusted to the darkness inside the building, he turned to see what it was and, to his astonishment, found all their kit, minus the weapons, piled up in a heap. So the terrorists had dumped it here and done nothing with it! He felt a surge of hope once again, but it was as quickly extinguished by the sound of shouting on the other side of the wall. They were getting closer.

Liam edged to the door and peered out through a crack in the wood. Azeez was yelling at his men, slapping some across the head, and pointing at the building where Liam had been held prisoner. Then a shot rang out and one of them dropped to the ground.

Liam knew then the decision had been made for him. His disappearance, and the guard's, had been discovered. And already someone had paid the ultimate price for the error. He had to go. Immediately.

As quietly as he could, he scrabbled around in the dark and found himself a bergen and webbing, quickly grabbing as much extra rations and water as he could from the other bags and stuffing them in. He then strapped himself in and edged back to the door – just as it was kicked open.

In front of him stood one of the terrorists, eyes filled with rage. His weapon was raised and ready to fire.

Liam's training took over, and before the figure in the door could register even a murmur of surprise he thrust the SCAR hard at his chest. If the bayonet met any resistance, it certainly didn't show it, and it sank in with the full length of its blade. With a twist, Liam heaved it back out and the man dropped to the ground in front of him.

Liam had no time to think about what had just happened and, quickly checking out beyond the door for the all clear, dashed out and round to the back of the building. With two terrorists now dead by his hand, he knew that being captured was not an option. His life would be snatched from him, no questions asked. And Azeez would probably enjoy making it a death both slow and horrific.

The dark Somali wilderness stared at him, daring him to venture into it. Not that he had any choice. It was either that, or head back and give himself up. Mind you, he could attempt to take on all the guards, perhaps steal the truck, play the hero everyone knows from the blockbuster movies. But you couldn't try that kind of crazy shit in real life.

Above him, the night was clear, the view of the stars stunning in such perfect darkness. And that, Liam realized, gave him an outside chance. In his belt kit somewhere would be a compass. With that, and the stars, he might be able to navigate his way back to the FOB. He'd also had basically the same escape and evasion training of anyone in the UKSF, so he had as good a chance as anyone of making it out of this alive.

Kicking his brain into gear, Liam dug deep to

remember what he could about star navigation, survival, staying hidden – even using moss on trees, as it would only ever be found on the south side of a trunk to catch the sun, to hazard a guess at his direction of travel. Then, with as good an idea as he was ever going to have about which direction to head in, he took one last look back to check no one was following him, then legged it, his first priority to get some distance between him and his captors.

When Liam eventually came to a stop, it was all he could do to not throw up. He'd pushed on through the pain barrier, telling himself again and again that the pain was just weakness leaving the body, and he kept going, sipping water as he went, thinking only of getting himself so far away from Abdul Azeez and his men, and probably so lost, that even if they did go looking for him, they'd never have a chance of finding him.

To escape detection, he had to avoid travelling during the day – to do so would only invite the inquisitive. And having already experienced the way folk seemed to just stroll off to have a cheeky spliff, he wasn't going to take any chances. So the further away he was, the better, and then he would be able to sort himself out a decent hide-away, stuff some cold rations into his face, and get some shut-eye. Trouble was, Liam knew that time was hardly playing him a fair hand. He estimated there was not much more than seventy-two hours left before the deadline was up and Azeez went to work with his SCAR. So it was a careful balance between ensuring his own survival, and getting a fucking move on. While it was still dark, he *had* to keep going.

The terrain was unforgiving, and with his eyes forever trying to keep lookout for the stars, tripping up was a hazard. And as he was staying away from any hint of human habitation, his journey was more often than not through ground untravelled. In the darkness, branches stretched towards him like claws. When on open ground, rocks and holes would appear out of nowhere to knock against his shin or swallow a foot and nearly snap his ankle. The quietness of the night seemed to amplify the noise of the wildlife all around him. If he stopped for a breather, it would sound as though creatures were nearby and closing in for a kill. Liam didn't stop for long, though. His entire focus was on survival and getting back to help rescue the rest of his section. If he didn't make it, none of them would.

After hours of travel, in what Liam hoped was the right direction, the night eventually began to fade and the golden glow of dawn spread with quiet inevitability.

Leaving it as long as he dared before stopping, Liam eventually decided to halt. He didn't want to be caught out with the sun fully in the sky, so he quickly got to work before it had a chance to even grab a peek at the world below.

The area around him reminded him very much of where he and the others had carried out their subsurface observations. This time, though, he wouldn't have the chance or the energy to dig a great big hole to hide in. Instead, he would have to make do with hiding himself deep inside some thick brush and hoping he was far enough away from any human habitation to avoid someone stumbling by for a peekaboo.

Out of sight, and as well camouflaged as he could hope for or achieve, Liam heaved himself into the doss bag pulled from his bergen. It was little less than five-star luxury compared to what he'd had to put up with since surrendering. Now on his belly, he ripped open a ration bag and ate ravenously, making absolutely sure that the empty bag was stowed safely away. He'd already learned that lesson during training, so he wasn't about to make the mistake again. Not here, for sure.

Despite the precarious nature of his predicament, Liam finally gave in to exhaustion and, as the sun climbed through the sky, he slept the dreamless sleep of the dead.

It was late afternoon when he finally stirred. He was

stunned by just how long he'd slept, with no waking in between. But after all he'd been through, it was no surprise. Given the chance to rest properly, his body and mind had snapped it up, though on waking he felt almost worse, his limbs stiff, his joints seized, and his mind already racing through what he was going to do next.

Moving deliberately slowly, just in case of the off chance that someone was out there and within earshot, Liam rolled over and peered through the gaps in the bush where he'd hidden. He filtered through everything he could hear. There was wind, there was wildlife, there was even the distant rumble of an aircraft tracing a line to its destination across the sky, but that was all. He was still alone.

He eased himself from his doss bag and, keeping low, was able to get a better idea of his surroundings. It had still been dark when he'd finally bedded down, so this was his first proper look-see at where he'd ended up. Initially it seemed much the same as everywhere else and his heart sank. What if all he'd been doing was walking in the wrong direction or, even worse, in circles? No, not circles, for he'd kept a compass bearing to follow – intelligence he hoped to be able to pass on to help with a rescue.

Then, far off, he spotted something. It was a range of

mountains, if such a grand word could be used to describe a collection of bare broken hills that sat together, jutting from the earth like long-forgotten skeletal remains. But what drew Liam's attention was that he was sure he recognized them. He stared hard for a few moments longer, trying to convince himself he was mistaken, but the more he looked the more he realized that he had seen them before. It had been while they were back at the FOB. And if Liam had experienced a sense of hope on managing to escape, he now felt elation. He had a definite place to aim for now that would, he was sure, help him find the rest of Recce Platoon and the KDF.

A target.

As darkness took root, Liam finally broke cover, slipping silently off into the night on a new compass bearing.

20

The night held little joy for Liam. Despite continually moving forwards, now with a destination firmly in mind, it seemed that with every step he barely moved at all. The air was thick, oily and sweet, and Liam found the quiet of the land around him disturbing. It was as though eyes were watching him, just waiting for him to make a mistake so they could come in for a kill. The sense of being prey rather than predator was only heightened by the howls of animals that seemed terrifyingly close.

Clammy with sweat, his clothes clung to him like clingfilm. Every step was painful. His feet weren't just sore, they were falling apart. He didn't want to risk pausing to check them, but could feel blisters swelling and bursting as he travelled on, the water and blood from inside them slipping between his toes and making them rub even more. When he wiped his forehead, sweat mixed with dust dripped into his eyes. It stung like hell.

Rationing his water was a constant mind battle when all he really wanted to do was sink pints of the stuff into his belly and pass out. And all the time his mind was filled with memories of what he'd gone through since being taken by Al Shabaab, of those he'd left behind, if they were even still alive.

But despite all of this, Liam wondered how long he would have survived if he hadn't chanced upon where their kit had been dumped. Not long at all, he guessed, and that was sobering, because he would have still had no choice but to make good his escape.

As dawn started to break, he was close to collapse. It was simply through force of will that he was still on his feet at all. He'd wanted to stop hours ago, but had kept on moving, the lives of his section always at the front of his mind. He had to keep going. There was no other choice.

After scouting the area, he chose somewhere to huddle away in. Trouble was, it didn't offer much in the way of natural cover; all he could find was an old tree trunk on its side. Drawing on his very last reserves of energy, he set to work scraping out a hollow beneath it, just deep enough for him to slip inside. Unable to do any more, Liam pushed his kit into the hollow, then scrabbled together armfuls of any dead vegetation he could find, stacking it around the tree in some attempt to disguise his hiding place. Then, with tiredness threatening to drop him where he stood, he slipped into the hole, pulled himself into his doss bag and muttered a desperate prayer, before once more giving in to the exhaustion that swept over him with the thunderous immediacy of an avalanche.

Voices.

At first, Liam thought a dream had woken him. Some memory playing itself out in his head while his body tried to recover. But when he heard them again, he knew it wasn't a dream – it was a real-life, honest to God nightmare.

The sun was dazzlingly bright and dust motes floated through the air. Liam lay absolutely still and quiet, once again terrified for his life. Now that it was light enough to review his hiding place properly, he was none too happy with what he'd achieved the night before. Yes, he was hidden, but even from where he was lying it looked artificial. It wouldn't take much for someone to walk by, wonder just what the hell had gone on and decide to come over for a closer look. If that happened they would see him for sure – and there he'd be, trapped in a doss bag, under a log, basically inviting people to come and slot him.

None of this was good. But there was little he could do, not with people milling about close by. If he broke cover, they would have him for sure. He had to edge himself out as quietly as possible, and hold onto hope.

With the voices still rumbling and chuntering away, Liam eased himself out of his doss bag as stealthily as possible. He then stuffed his kit back inside the bergen, and made sure the SCAR was to hand. It wouldn't be much use in such cramped conditions, but if he had to bolt then a burst from the barrel would at least have his pursuers' heads down and make them think twice about keeping up with the chase.

Wanting to get eyes on what he might be facing, Liam slid up to the top of the hole to have a nosy. After all, he thought, he could be worrying about nothing, just some farmer going about his business.

With the SCAR in front of him, he crawled upwards and stared hard through the rough vegetation he'd laid down over his hiding place. It was difficult to see at first, the bright light forcing his eyes shut and making them water. But once they'd cleared his heart sank. A farmer he could deal with, but this? This was a worst-case scenario and little more than twenty metres away.

How he had missed it? He'd been exhausted, close to collapse, but blind? It didn't matter now. He had a situation to deal with and focusing on how it had happened wasn't going to help at all.

A rough track cut across in front of him, not close enough to touch, but a few steps further and he would be able to thumb a lift back to Abdul Azeez. Just beyond that was a collection of buildings. Rough dwellings, one storey in height, and standing in front of them, chatting away and sharing bottles of Coke, was a group of armed men. He counted at least fifteen, all armed with everything from AKs to AR15s, with a few RPGs thrown in for good measure.

Liam cursed his bad luck. To have come so far and to not yet be caught, and then to end up bedding down just spitting distance away from another bunch of Al Shabaab nutters seemed wholly unfair. But on the bright side, at least they hadn't stumbled on him while he was still asleep. Now, at least he had the upper hand. He knew where they were, but they had no idea about him. Not yet. And if he kept quiet and they didn't get spooked by anything, come nightfall he would have a decent chance of slipping away undiscovered.

For a while Liam held his position, observing the men from his hole. They seemed relaxed, happy even. Perhaps even terrorists had days off, he thought, and almost smiled at the idea. Despite everything, his humour didn't fail him. Then, as he made to slip back down into the darkness of his hideaway, the metallic clatter of automatic rifle fire tore the day apart as one of the terrorists was kicked backwards by a spray of rounds that took apart his chest. A shot of adrenaline blasted through Liam and had his heart rate up in a second. Quickly, he shuffled back out of the hole to see what was going on, hoping with everything he had left that it was nothing to do with him.

What had been a calm, relaxed scene was now all action and violence. The terrorists were firing wildly from behind the buildings, yelling at each other, looking for ways to bolt. But who the hell were they fighting? Each other?

Liam narrowed his eyes to fend off the glare of the sun, tracing their line of fire to try and see who was coming in on an attack. One of the terrorists made a break for it, pegging it across the road and towards him. Liam immediately had the SCAR up and ready to fire, but the man was kicked into the air as rounds slammed into him, dropping him just a metre or so away from Liam's hole.

Controlling his breathing, forcing himself not to panic, Liam stayed where he was. Whoever was coming in at Al Shabaab wasn't messing around. And then he caught sight of them.

He recognized the fatigues immediately. It was the

ANDY McNAB

KDF, and judging by the amount of fire coming in, at least a platoon's worth of them. At first Liam was relieved, but then he realized this could just as easily turn bad for him too. The Kenyans had no idea he was there. For all he knew, they were a group who had nothing at all to do with the ones he had worked with back at BATUK and at the FOB. In the confusion of the battle raging in front of him, it wouldn't take much for them to stumble on him and take him out before realizing he wasn't actually Al Shabaab. And there was also the issue of stray bullets. The air was thick with rounds as the KDF closed in. If he made a break for it there was always an outside chance one would find him.

Liam kept his head down. The fighting was upping in intensity as the KDF moved closer. The Al Shabaab terrorists were outgunned and outnumbered, but they were fighting back hard. Rounds were peppering the ground, slamming into the buildings, smashing rock and stone. Liam could hear the whine of ricochets. Then at last, realizing their cause was lost, some of the terrorists started to make a break for freedom, racing off hard into the surrounding countryside.

He stayed hidden: with things becoming so desperate he didn't want to risk anything now there was a chance he could survive the battle and, hopefully, somehow communicate with the KDF.

The sound of running feet caught Liam's attention, but before he had a chance to react a figure tripped and, with a shocked yell, fell down into the scrape next to him. For a moment the two of them stared at each other, both as shocked as the other at the turn of events. Then, with panic wild in his eyes, the terrorist tried to aim his weapon at Liam, but there wasn't enough room. When the man brought it to bear, the weapon caught on the tree trunk above them as he pulled the trigger, and rounds thumped harmlessly into the wood, covering them both in dagger-like splinters.

Liam, fully aware that his SCAR would only hinder him in the claustrophobic hole they were both in, threw himself at his assailant, knocking the weapon to one side and powering into him with his fists. What training he'd received in hand-to-hand combat had never covered anything like this and every second was desperate. The man fought back, slamming Liam hard across the face with the back of his hand, but Liam hardly noticed. He was on top of him now, struggling to maintain the advantage as he continued his attack. The sudden explosive aggression had him breathing hard and he knew that if he didn't close this down sharpish, fatigue would get the better of him.

A glint of metal caught his eye and Liam saw the man pull out a knife with his left hand. He slashed with it, catching Liam's arm, but the attack was wild and uncontrolled and Liam managed to grab hold of the man's arm and pin it under his knee. He immediately followed this with a crushing head-butt, breaking his attacker's nose, and then went back in with a flurry of punches. Most missed their target, but those that connected did so with terrible power.

Liam felt the man beneath him go limp. Then, as he raised his fist to make absolutely sure he wasn't going to wake up any time soon, a shout stopped him short.

He looked up and found himself staring down a barrel.

21

'How long have I been gone?'

Liam's question was directed at Lieutenant Young, who was sitting with him in a tent back at the FOB. It wasn't exactly private health care, but considering what he had been through, the medics had done a top job of checking him thoroughly and he almost felt human. Before he'd even been fully debriefed on what had happened – though he'd immediately passed on the essential rough intelligence he'd gathered about where the hostages were being held – he'd been jabbed with numerous needles, all filled with drugs designed to hunt and kill any possible infection he might have contracted during his ordeal. His feet had been checked and dressed and, thankfully, weren't as bad as they had initially suspected. The cuts had been cleaned out and he had even been able to have a shower. Now he was in clean clothes, resting on a bed, and attached to a drip to get his fluids back up. He had also been brought a good supply of hot, sweet tea and some scoff to get down his neck.

'Twelve days,' said the lieutenant. 'And nobody here has slept in that time. But then neither has the Prime Minister, courtesy of those videos you were all forced to make.'

'The Prime Minister?' said Liam, sipping from his mug. Usually he hated sugar in his drinks, but this stuff tasted like nectar. The warmth of it flowed through his body and the sweetness was the most delicious thing he'd ever had in his life.

'Eight men go missing, that's a big deal,' said Young. 'And it still has the potential to be the biggest political shit storm you could imagine. We have had offers from across the globe to help find you and bring you out.'

'Didn't know we were that important,' said Liam.

'This is the British Army, Scott. Of course you're important!' The lieutenant smiled and Liam laughed.

'Well, we are the best, right, sir?'

'That's a given,' the lieutenant said. 'Now, we're working on the INT you've already handed over, but tell me in detail what happened? Captain Owusu – indeed, everyone here – is good and ready to head in and get the rest of the lads out. And with that deadline just round the corner we need to move right now.'

'Me too,' said Liam.

Young didn't comment.

'The KDF lads thought I was one of the terrorists,' said Liam. 'They were geed up from the firefight and it took just a little too long to make them realize that I wasn't Al Shabaab.'

'Well, you looked a fucking mess, in all honesty, Scott. And you stank to high heaven. We've burned your clothes.'

'Pity,' said Liam. 'There was a few months left in them.'

'So,' Young pressed, 'what actually happened? We heard nothing for days following your disappearance after the KDF assault.'

'Yeah, that went to shit,' said Liam. 'Some guy from the KDF switched sides was what we heard.'

'It was a mess,' said Young. 'It's made everyone realize that Al Shabaab aren't just a bunch of fanatical nutjobs looking for a glorious death. They're cunning and ruthless. No pushover.'

'Wait till you meet Azeez,' said Liam. 'He makes the rest of them look like nursery teachers.'

At this, the lieutenant's face grew dark. 'He has carved himself quite the reputation for ruthlessness,' he said.

Liam nodded, then reported everything that had happened from the moment they'd surrendered. At the mention of the KDF prisoners the lieutenant spoke.

'Courtesy of Al Jazeera, the videos went viral,' he said. 'Not just the footage of you lads, but also another film they made of the KDF hostages. Azeez was clearly over the moon with grabbing you lot. Best PR exercise he could hope for.'

'They moved us to a place with cages,' said Liam. 'Food and water twice a day. The KDF soldiers looked the worst, though.'

'And now here you are,' said Young. 'They'll write books about you, Scott. What you've achieved is nothing short of superhuman.'

'Bollocks is it,' said Liam. 'I got out and the rest of the lads are still in the hands of Al Shabaab. For all I know, they're dead.'

'Well, we don't think they are, not yet anyway. Azeez has been on the charm offensive. Released another home movie.'

Liam sat up. 'What?'

'It shows the body of a dead soldier. One who apparently tried to escape.'

'Carter?'

Young shook his head. 'Hair was the wrong colour,' he said. 'So after what you've told me I'm thinking it was one of Azeez's own, stripped of his clothes and dressed in some of the kit you lads had with you.'

'So they're alive?'

'We don't know for sure,' said Young. 'But we think Abdul Azeez is holding onto his prizes. Killing them would do little for his cause. If he can parade them about, he probably thinks he's showing the world just how powerful he is.'

Liam stared hard at the lieutenant. 'So what are we going to do to make him realize that he isn't?'

Liam stared at a map and a number of black and white aerial photographs in front of him. With him were Lieutenant Young and Captain Owusu.

'From everything you've told us – some very good INT by the way in the circs, Scott,' said the lieutenant, 'we were able to get a fly-by from some very willing RAF lads happy to take a few holiday snaps.'

The photographs showed a collection of buildings and a track.

'And I must say,' said the lieutenant, 'the drawings you gave us were rather good. We've compared them with these photographs, and the map, and we're pretty certain we've nailed the location.'

Liam laughed. 'The sarge won't believe that when he gets back,' he said. 'Reckons my pencil skills are crap.'

'Well, clearly not any more,' said the lieutenant and dropped his finger onto one of the photographs. 'This is the compound,' he explained. 'It's bigger than on your sketches, but seems to fit your description. And this here is a vehicle. A large one, a truck of some kind.'

Liam leaned in for a closer look, comparing it with what he could remember of where he had been held prisoner in a cage with the rest of the section. It looked bigger than he remembered, more buildings, but it had been night when they arrived, and night when he did a runner, so he hadn't grasped the whole layout. But there was enough there to tell him what he needed to know.

'That's it,' he said. 'No doubt about it.'

'You're sure?' asked Owusu.

Liam nodded. 'That's the latrine,' he said, pointing at a structure behind one of the buildings. 'It's also the last resting place of the drunken guard. And that's the truck we were transported in.' He checked through the other photographs. 'It looks busy,' he said, noticing stationary figures around the buildings. 'There weren't many guarding us when I was there. I think they thought it was an easy job, no chance of us causing any grief.'

'Well, they've changed their mind,' said Young. 'Or at least, Azeez has. We've counted upwards of forty men.'

'And which building are the rest of the section held in?' asked the captain.

'That one,' said Liam without hesitation, his finger

again on one of the photographs. 'I can remember that because of the route from it to the latrine.' He looked up at the two officers. 'So are we going in?'

'Well, we're certainly not going to sit around here discussing the weather,' said the captain. 'With your gallant escape we now have a chance to make good a rescue. However, time is of the essence. Although he will almost certainly believe you to be dead by now, Mr Abdul Azeez will be rather irritated, I should think, to have lost you, and I am definitely of the opinion that the sooner we get our men out, the better. Before Azeez gets any other ideas.'

'So when do we go?'

'Everyone is already set,' said the lieutenant. 'The compound the lads are held in isn't exactly accessible. A land insertion would take too long and could ultimately fail. So we are going in with a direct aerial assault.'

'You mean a smash and grab?'

The captain nodded. 'Speed, aggression, surprise. We go in fast, hit them hard, grab our boys, and get the hell out.'

Liam was impressed. A part of him had been worrying that there would be a delay, that perhaps the powers that be wouldn't want to go in straight away because of the risks involved. But the captain and lieutenant were clearly far ahead with the rescue plan.

Liam stood up. 'I'll get myself ready,' he said, but Young's hand reached for him and made him sit back down.

'Listen, Scott,' he said. 'You've already been to hell and back. You were a mess when we found you. God knows what kind of stress you've suffered. We think—'

'You think what? That I'm not fit to go?'

The lieutenant remained silent.

'Well, bollocks to that, sir. I'm going in.'

'We have men all ready to go,' explained Owusu. 'It is better that you rest, recuperate.'

'You really expect me to sit back here with my feet up while you all go in to get them out? No fucking way!'

'You have to understand—' said Young, but Liam cut him short.

'I know that place better than any of you,' he said. 'You need me on the ground – I can lead you right to the prisoners. What's the point of having my eyes back here when they could help with the attack? It doesn't make sense!'

'And neither does going in there intent on revenge,' said the captain.

'That's not what this is about, sir,' said Liam, fighting to remain calm. 'I got out, and in doing so had to leave them behind. There's no way in hell that I'm staying back here. And anyway,' he added, 'Fish is still out of action, right?'

Young shrugged. 'Yes,' he said. 'And pretty pissed off about it.'

'Then you're a man down after Azeez murdered Carter. I'm going in instead of Fish or Carter.'

Captain Owusu and Lieutenant Young stared at each other and eventually nodded.

'You're not going to let this rest, are you?' asked Young.

'It's my section,' said Liam. 'They'd do the same for me.'

'Then you're in,' said the captain. 'But you have to promise me one thing.'

'Of course, sir,' said Liam, wondering just what kind of request Captain Owusu was going to put to him.

'The latrine,' he said. 'If it's all the same with you, I'd prefer it if you didn't dump any more bodies down there. If you do, you can bloody well go and fish them out yourself.'

22

It was mid-afternoon and Liam went through a final check of his kit. No bergen this time, and he was pleased about that. Instead, he had his battle kit on and was bombed up with over three hundred rounds for his SA80, two hundred additional link rounds for his machine gun, phosphorous grenades, four high explosive fragmentation grenades, a field medical kit and a camel bak to keep him hydrated.

He'd handed back the SCAR rifle to the KDF and was now once again armed with an SA80 and side arm, the Glock. He'd been half tempted to keep hold of the SCAR, but he knew the SA80 inside and out. He'd used one countless times and could depend on it. Going into a hot situation with a new weapon wasn't sensible. And looking cool didn't keep you alive.

Around him, the rest of Recce Platoon were as restless as him – even Fish, despite not being able to go out on the ground. However, he wasn't exactly a spare part, staying back at the FOB to work the radio comms. This was no ordinary mission. They were going in to rescue their own. And they were all raring to get to it sharpish.

Lieutenant Young called everyone together and a hush fell immediately, everyone quiet, not wanting to miss a word. They had already gone through what the operation involved and what they would be doing, so this was the final briefing to clarify it and make absolutely sure everyone knew the facts.

'To recap, the situation is as follows,' said the lieutenant, his voice commanding and measured. 'We have six of the original eight-man section currently held hostage by Abdul Azeez. In addition, we have four surviving KDF hostages. One of ours is already confirmed dead; the other is Lance Corporal Scott, who managed through some quite extraordinary efforts on his part to escape. It is thanks to him that we are able to do what I'm hoping Azeez thinks is practically impossible – go in and get our lads the hell out.'

There was a murmur of agreement, which quickly roused into cheers of 'Too bloody right' and 'Absofucking-lutely'.

'One other soldier is injured,' continued the lieutenant, 'but only superficially. However, under the conditions of his confinement, there is every chance that he will be immobile.'

Liam thought about Bale. He'd been lucky to receive only a graze from the bullet: it could just as easily have smashed through his leg, caught a main artery, and had him bleed out. But they had all been lucky. Azeez could have slaughtered them on the spot.

'Everyone listen in,' said the lieutenant. 'Mission: to release the hostages. Mission: to release the hostages.'

Liam knew that the way the lieutenant had just spoken would sound odd to a civilian, but the reason a mission statement was said twice was so that everyone understood exactly what they were about to do. Once on the ground, everything they did would be to achieve that goal and advance the mission. Nothing else mattered.

'We go in, we find them, and we get them out,' continued the lieutenant. 'That is our objective. Anything else that happens is a by-product of this. And by that, I mean the apprehension of Abdul Azeez.'

'You mean we can't nab the bastard?' called out one of the soldiers.

'That's not exactly what I said,' replied the lieutenant with a wry smile. 'So if we happen to apprehend him in the process, all well and good. But it is not the priority.'

Liam understood this completely. If a mission had two objectives there was a good chance that confusion on the ground could lead to both objectives being screwed. Focus on one, and there was a much better chance of it being successful. And by stating it loud and clear, the lieutenant was making absolutely sure that everyone knew what they were doing and when they were doing it, as well as why.

'As you all know, we will be going in as a direct aerial assault,' continued the lieutenant. 'There will be enough daylight to make finding the hostages easier and to minimize the risk of any blue on blue. Fire support will be provided by a Lynx Mark 7 attack helicopter. The KDF, with our support, will draw out Al Shabaab and distract them. This will enable us to send in a team to secure the hostages, then get them the fuck out and into the Chinooks. It will be a fast-rope insertion, so remember your gloves. Firing a weapon with your hands half melted is no fun at all.'

Everyone knew the reputation of the Lynx. Holding the world air-speed record for helicopters, it was armed with miniguns. Loaded with 7.62 rounds, they could spit fire out at a rate of between two and six thousand rounds per minute. And if you got in the way of that, there was no getting up again.

As for the fast-rope insertion, it was something Liam had done in training but never for real. And each time it had been pretty bloody exciting. With only his hands to slow him down – the use of boots was not advised as boot polish could scrape off onto the rope and make it dangerously slippery for those coming after you – he and the rest of the lads would exit the helicopters via a 40mm thick braided rope. It was fast, which meant the helicopter could drop its load and get out sharpish, and also pretty risky. But it worked, and so long as everyone was wearing gloves, as the lieutenant had just reminded them, Liam figured it made total sense. Speed, surprise and aggression were the foundation stones of the operation and a fast-rope insertion was the natural choice.

'We will drop in plenty of smoke to cover our advance, and will go in hard and fast,' Lieutenant Young concluded. 'We'll get out just as quickly.'

As the lieutenant finished speaking, the distant thrum of twin helicopter engines buffeted in on the wind. Liam recognized them immediately as the rotors of a Chinook and soon spotted two helicopters heading their way. Tailing them was the Lynx. Seeing them approach gave Liam a boost of confidence in the mission ahead. If it all went according to plan, Azeez and his pals really wouldn't have a clue what had hit them.

Briefing over, everyone gathered themselves together, ready for the off. Liam was with Lieutenant Young, Corporal Slater – 'Bull' – and Lance Corporal Parker.

The lieutenant pulled Liam, Slater and Parker aside.

'We've been through this already, but it doesn't hurt anyone to go through it again. So, Slater?'

'Lieutenant?'

'Give us a run-through.'

Liam wasn't small, but standing next to Slater made him feel tiny. The man's shadow was so big it could create its own microclimate, he thought.

'Our job is to find and secure the hostages,' said Bull. 'With the KDF drawing fire from one direction, we – with fire support from the rest of Recce Platoon – will be using RB here as our search dog to locate the hostages. And we'll be going in on the Lynx, which if you ask me, is fucking blinding!'

'You don't get to use the miniguns, though,' said Parker. 'That's the pilot's job, Bull. Sorry, mate.'

'He'll let me have a go, surely,' said Slater. 'I'll be careful.'

'That's what the bull said just before it went to buy a dinner set,' quipped the lieutenant.

'The nickname suits him,' said Parker.

'Well then,' said Lieutenant Young, 'what say we hitch a ride and get shifting?'

Behind them, the rest of Recce Platoon were loading up into one of the Chinooks, with a platoon from the KDF into the other. As Liam and the others jogged over to the Lynx, Liam caught sight of a figure legging it towards them. It was Odull. He was supposed to be jumping into one of the Chinooks, not racing over to the Lynx.

'Who the hell's that?' asked Slater.

'Odull,' said Liam. 'Had two brothers. One's dead, the other is one of the KDF hostages.'

'Fuck.'

'Exactly.'

In all that had happened, Liam had almost forgotten about the big Kenyan and his own personal reason to get Abdul Azeez. If this went well, he thought, then he'd make sure to go and have a decent chat with him afterwards. Odull was a good man and Liam already knew he was the kind of soldier he would happily fight alongside any day.

Odull stopped in front of him. 'I wish to come with you. I must be there for my brother. It is my duty.'

Lieutenant Young stepped in. 'Odull, your place is with the rest of the KDF. So get back there, sharpish!'

Odull shook his head. 'The KDF soldiers who are prisoners – their English is bad. Also, they will trust me. Perhaps, after so long as prisoners, they will not trust you? But if they see my face—'

'Absolutely not,' said Young. 'You're too close to this. We can't risk you going off on some personal mission.'

Odull turned his attention to Liam. He did not speak, but his eyes said everything that was on his mind.

'I think Odull has a point,' said Liam. 'I've been there, sir, and it is a shit hole. Those KDF lads are in a real mess. We can't afford for them to go crazy on us. Odull is a guarantee that they'll know we're the good guys.'

Young paused for a moment, then glanced at Slater and Parker. 'And your thoughts on this?'

'Fine by me, sir,' said Slater. 'Big lad like Odull running with us can only be good, right?'

With a nod, Young turned to Odull and ran through what they were going to do. 'Clear?'

'Sir,' said Odull, grinning wide.

'Good,' said Young, then handed Odull a spare of gloves he was carrying. 'You'll be needing these!'

And with that, they all clambered into the back of the Lynx.

Sitting in the helicopter, Liam focused on his breathing, calming himself for what lay ahead. Opposite him was Parker, who stared out through the open side of the helicopter, probably writing a poem in his head as part of his preparation routine. Slater was just sitting there like a massive happy ape, and Lieutenant Young was eyes on the Chinooks. As for Odull, Liam could see the determination set in his jaw. This was a man going to rescue his brother and Liam sensed that there was little Al Shabaab could do to stop him.

Then the two big Chinooks took to the sky, and like a bird of prey the Lynx upped and followed.

Keeping low, at points barely metres above the tree line, the Chinooks and the Lynx chopped their way through the air. A trek that had taken Liam days to walk would now last less than half an hour. Even if they were spotted and a message was passed along through the Al Shabaab communication line, they'd be on with the attack before anything could be done about it.

Liam was sitting in the cabin of the helicopter, the wind gusting in and keeping him cool. He ran over the plan again in his mind, taking a step-by-step walk through the compound they were approaching, making sure every bit of it was absolutely clear. It had to be. In the confusion of their attack, and the smoke that would be dropped to cover them, they all needed to know exactly where they were going.

A signal from the co-pilot came through. With a thumbs up all round, they knew they were only a couple of minutes away from going in. There was no point trying to communicate on the PRRs as all sound was drowned out by the rotor engine above their heads.

Slater got ready with the rope for the fast insertion as

Liam, Parker, Odull and the lieutenant checked their gloves were on good and tight. They would be ripped off on landing as the descent would render them useless and trigger feel was always better against bare fingers than through a glove. The co-pilot would then haul the rope back into the cabin.

Liam noticed the telltale change in the sound of the engines as the Lynx pulled itself into a hover. With a nod from the lieutenant, Slater dropped the rope. They were poised at approximately ten metres up. A fall from this height was out of the question unless you wanted a broken back. Then, leading the way, Lieutenant Young was out of the helicopter and sliding down the rope. Liam followed, and behind him came Parker, then Slater, with Odull bringing up the rear. It took fifteen seconds to get them all onto the ground.

Now it was time to rescue his mates.

23

Running forward with four other heavily armed soldiers, Liam watched as the Lynx unleashed hell, opening up the miniguns on the truck that had transported him and the rest of the section to their prison. A number of other vehicles had since joined it, and they suffered the same fate. The rounds tore into them with abandon, ripping them to shreds. When the fuel tanks were hit by the searingly hot metal, they were sent skyward as the liquid ignited. He caught sight of the Chinooks held in hover, ropes down, men zipping out and onto the ground like wasps racing from a nest. Once they were out, Liam knew the aircraft would hop to a safe distance then come back for a pick-up when called.

'Knock knock,' said Slater across the PRR as they lobbed in a few phosphorous grenades to add some smoke to the confusion.

The Lynx pulled away as the KDF and the rest of Recce Platoon advanced.

The plan was simple. With confusion brought on by the attack from the Lynx, the KDF would draw the fire of the terrorists by attacking them from one direction. This would allow Liam's squad, and the rest of Recce Platoon, to swoop in, deal with any threat and rescue the hostages. And with the element of surprise, it was hoped the terrorists would be too confused to have time to think while they led the hostages away and got them into the Chinooks and the fuck out of there.

Liam spotted the latrine and guessed the guard was probably still down there somewhere, his body being slowly preserved by the huge amounts of shit he was covered in. He quickly signalled to the others as from round the corner of one of the buildings a group of gunmen appeared. Liam counted five, four of whom were armed with AK47s, the fifth with one of the KDF's SCARs. They were all firing from the hip.

Liam dropped to his knee and had his SA80 up into the shoulder. To his left, the lieutenant, Slater and Parker did the same. On his right, Odull followed suit, fitting in with natural ease to their first live contact as, with short sharp three-round bursts, they all opened fire.

The man with the SCAR was hit first, spinning

backwards and away from his mates like a puppet cut from its strings.

Liam brought his barrel round to bear on another of the men when movement caught his eye. Far off to his right, hidden by some bushes, was a shadow. He swung his weapon round and, staring through the sight, got eyes on what he'd seen. It took a split second for him to make out a silhouette that didn't belong. And it was definitely human. He stared a moment longer and registered an immediate threat. The figure was holding a weapon. And it wasn't a rifle.

'RPG!' Liam yelled 'Two o'clock! One hundred!'

Odull switched his attack and hammered the bushes with a rapid succession of bursts from his rifle. A flash of light exploded from where Liam had spotted the figure and they all ducked instinctively as the RPG blasted out like an expensive firework. But it wasn't heading towards them. Instead, it swung off wildly and piled into the men who had come to attack them. None of the terrorists registered its approach and it hammered into the ground directly amongst them. The explosion kicked dust, rock, stone and the shattered remains of the terrorists high into the air, disintegrating the men in an instant. It wasn't pretty, but it was certainly effective.

'I think I got him,' said Odull across the PRR.

'And the others,' said Liam.

With the threat dealt with, they moved again. Around them other battles were raging as the KDF engaged with the terrorists, and the rest of Recce Platoon provided targeted fire support for Liam and his team. Some terrorists were trying to make a break for it, but there was nowhere to run to and they were met with a resistance that had them pinned down.

Liam was up and moving forward towards the buildings, the others slipping in behind him. Lieutenant Young might have held rank over them all, but Liam knew the ground and that put him on point. The others trusted him and that made him work his soldiering skills even harder. He wasn't going to fuck this up.

Two men ran out in front of Liam, both firing wildly at nothing in particular, screaming and yelling with rage. Liam had his rifle up and took the first down, but as he moved onto the other his rifle clicked empty.

'Magazine!' Liam shouted as he dropped to the ground, making himself harder to hit while he changed mags, while also allowing the rest of the lads a clearer arc of fire. Slater was on the other gunman in a beat, shattering his chest with a calmly fired clatter of rounds.

Up on his feet again, Liam led on, past the two dead terrorists and on towards the latrine. The smell was thick in the air, filling it with a rotting foulness that was hard to ignore. He pushed on, quashing the memory of what had happened there the last time he'd passed by.

Liam came up alongside the building where he had hidden in the moments before his escape. Just beyond it, in the central area surrounded by the other buildings, smoke was billowing out from the vehicles destroyed by the Lynx.

Keeping himself tight to the building and edging left, Liam continued to lead the way, with Lieutenant Young behind him, followed in quick succession by Slater, Parker and Odull. He could hear them breathing, but it wasn't out of exhaustion. They were all fit and this was what they trained for. They were alert and Liam knew he couldn't be with better men.

A scuffle came from behind them, and as Liam shot a look down the line he saw Parker swing round at the back and drop another terrorist whose AK47 sprayed wildly into the air as he fell backwards.

Liam raised a hand, halting their advance. About ten metres across from him was a section of open ground, and beyond that was the makeshift prison. Liam hoped to whatever God might exist that its occupants were still alive and that his escape hadn't caused their execution.

Liam lobbed a couple of phosphorous grenades into the gap, filling it immediately with thick grey smoke. He then nodded to the lieutenant to give covering fire and dashed across, slamming into the wall of the prison.

Dropping to his knee, he then opened up with covering fire and the lieutenant, Parker, Slater and Odull quickly joined him.

'They're in here,' said Liam across the PRR, knocking the wall with his fist. 'There's only one door in and out, and that's round the front.'

'Then let's not hang about here chinwagging,' said the lieutenant.

Liam led the way once again, and with the grey smoke from the grenades dancing around them like phantoms, they moved swiftly round the corner of the building and along its front, quickly coming up against the door.

Liam made to kick it down when it was suddenly pulled open. Another terrorist ran out, firing as he went. The rounds weren't aimed but it was enough to make them drop to the ground. Then Parker had him in his sights and eliminated any further threat with a three-round burst that caught the terrorist in the face.

Slater held his position, covering the door, while the others moved into the building. The cages were still there – as was the stink.

'Holy fuck, it's the cavalry,' came an all too familiar voice.

'Nice to see you too, Pearce,' said Liam, running over to his cage and knocking the lock clean off with the butt of his rifle. The lieutenant and the other two Recce soldiers did the same, moving quickly from cage to cage to release the others. Odull ran straight over to his brother and the other KDF lads.

'We all thought you'd gone for a take-out, RB,' Pearce said. 'I could murder a good curry.'

Down the line, the rest of the section were edging out of their cages. They looked even worse than Liam had remembered. Stiff and bent over, thanks to their cramped conditions, they looked like the human versions of the pitiful dogs used in adverts by the RSPCA. Liam caught sight of Odull – the door to his brother's cage had been ripped clean off and the two men were embracing. It didn't last long, but it was enough to show the bond that only brothers can ever know.

'Come on,' said Liam, gesturing to Pearce to get off his arse. 'We need to shift it.'

'No can do,' said Pearce, and Liam knew immediately from the tone of his voice that he wasn't joking. He quickly ducked inside Pearce's cage.

'What's wrong?'

'Got myself a good beating,' said Pearce. 'I tell you what, RB, these Al Shabaab fuckers have no sense of humour.'

'I warned him,' came another voice, and Liam turned

to find himself staring at Cordner. 'Jokes about pies just don't translate.'

'I found them fucking hilarious,' said Pearce.

'Exactly,' said Cordner. 'And that should be warning enough.'

'Still coping without the fags?' Liam asked.

'Mate, if I'd never smoked in my life, after an experience like this, I'd be taking it up.'

Liam quickly checked Pearce over. He looked worse than the others. Whereas they were dirty, at least their cuts and bruises had faded – Pearce looked like he'd just got into an argument with a grizzly bear.

'Can you walk?'

Pearce shook his head. 'The bastards stamped on my left ankle. Probably broken. The fucker's so swollen it's close to bursting out of my boot.'

Lieutenant Young took control. 'Pearce and Bale need carrying,' he said.

'Waterman?' asked Liam.

'Just point me in the right direction and I'm there,' came Waterman's reply from somewhere in the dark.

'Odull has the KDF lads under control,' said Young. 'I'll take point with Parker. Scott, you bring up the rear. Slater, you grab Pearce.'

Liam saw a familiar figure step forward. It was Sergeant Biggs. 'I'll do that,' he said, 'if only to get the bastard to buy me a beer when we get home. Slater can grab Bale.'

'It's just take, take, take with you, isn't it?' said Pearce. 'Besides, you owe me one after we had to lug your fat arse around.'

Cordner stepped up next to the sergeant. 'Seems like the first round is yours, mate,' he said. 'Come on, Biggsy, let's get his sorry arse out of here.'

Liam edged back as the sergeant and Cordner carefully helped Pearce out of the cage, then had him lean across their shoulders, spreading his weight.

'The extraction point is being covered by the rest of the Recce lads,' said the lieutenant. 'When we leave the cover of this building, we shift it. No stopping for souvenirs or holiday snaps.'

'Bit unfair,' said Pearce. 'What am I going to show the wife when I get back?'

'You don't have a wife,' said Biggs.

'That's it,' said Pearce. 'Hit a man while he's down.'

Lieutenant Young called everyone to order. 'We move on my mark!'

The men shifted into a line.

'Go!'

Moving out through the door, the lieutenant led the way back along the edge of the building, the rest of the Recce lads following behind in quick succession.

Odull and the KDF were in the middle of the huddle, the big Kenyan hoisting one of the KDF prisoners – a man clearly in a bad way – onto his shoulders while his brother helped another to limp to freedom. At the back, Liam was alert and looking for potential threats. So far so good; the KDF had clearly done their job, and with the support of Recce Platoon, the terrorists had been cleared out. He had no doubt, though, that there were still a few stragglers hanging on. Another thing that was bothering him was the whereabouts of the kingpin of the whole thing, Abdul Azeez. Just where in hell was he?

Out of nowhere an RPG blasted past Liam, just missing the line of men in front of him. It hammered into the wall of the building opposite, the one where their kit had been hidden. The wall didn't put up much of a fight as the warhead took it apart, spraying everyone with shards of rubble and clouds of dust, knocking most of them to the ground.

Liam coughed, wiped grit from his face and tried to stare ahead through eyes watering painfully. He looked at the rest of the soldiers with him. They were covered in dust and some were bloodied, others shaking their heads, stunned by the explosion. Then, to his right, Liam glimpsed a figure approaching through the smoke. He wasn't running, but walking almost nonchalantly, like he hadn't a care in the world. The smoke cleared and

Liam saw the face of his nemesis. Azeez had been here all along.

Grabbing his rifle, Liam brought it round and pulled the trigger, but for the first time ever, his weapon jammed. With no time to try and sort it, and with the prisoners and the rest of his squad as yet unaware of Azeez, Liam jumped to his feet and threw himself at the self-proclaimed prince of Al Shabaab.

Azeez, taken by surprise, tried to dodge, but wasn't quick enough and Liam caught him in the chest with his head, his helmet lending added impact. The terrorist leader was thrown backwards by the force of Liam's attack and stumbled. He tried to bring his weapon round, but Liam kept on pushing and then they both dropped, Azeez falling backwards, Liam on top of him.

Liam raised himself up to straddle Azeez. Still half blind after the RPG, he went in hard and wild with his fists, but Azeez came back at him, blocking the punches and then reaching beneath his bloodied tunic.

Out came an evil-looking blade. The glint of metal caught Liam's eye. Knife fights were the one thing you never got into. They were nothing like how they were portrayed in the movies, but instead were short, violent and bloody. Liam had to deal with it before Azeez skewered him.

He grabbed the wrist holding the knife with both hands. Azeez struggled, but Liam had the advantage of being on top. He rocked himself forward, forcing Azeez's hand above his head. Then, as the terrorist's hand touched the ground, he drove in hard with his helmet again, head-butting Azeez in the face.

Liam pulled himself up to come in hard again, but one look at Azeez told him it wasn't necessary. The smile was gone and the eyes were closed. Abdul Azeez was out cold.

He rolled the Al Shabaab leader onto his front, snapped his wrists together with a plastic tie from one of his pouches, then scrambled to his feet and hoisted the still unconscious man onto his shoulders. Then he was back in the line with the others, who though dazed were up and ready to get the hell out.

'Come on, let's shift it!' he yelled out. 'Move!'

From the front, Lieutenant Young led them onwards, and they headed off through the dust and smoke. Liam kept his eyes on Slater in front of him, ignoring the weight of the body now across his shoulders. His legs were burning, his eyes stinging, but the welcome sound of a Chinook's twin propellers kept him moving onwards. Then the downed ramp of the helicopter appeared and before he realized what he was doing, Liam was inside and dropping Abdul Azeez to the floor.

271

Coming in behind him were the rest of the Recce Platoon.

Liam grabbed a seat and buckled up. Opposite him, Pearce was quickly strapped in by Sergeant Biggs and Cordner. They all stared at the comatose body of Abdul Azeez on the deck of the Chinook.

Pearce caught his eye and winked. 'Thanks, RB,' he mouthed across the rattle and hum of the engines.

Then Liam's stomach churned as the Chinook lifted off.

24

Liam was standing to attention with the rest of Recce Platoon and the KDF back at BATUK. In front of them a Chinook waited for its cargo, the loading bay open, rotors stilled. Silence reigned.

In front of the soldiers, lying on a simple platform of two trestles and a plank of wood, was a box draped in the Union Jack. Inside lay the body of Carter. In a search of the area to flush out more Al Shabaab terrorists, the KDF had found his remains and brought him back. Though the loss of one of their own had hit them hard, they were all relieved that he had been found – it had been unthinkable that they might have to leave his body behind and be unable to award him the respect he deserved.

Six men walked forwards and lined up, three down either side of the coffin, with Lieutenant Young standing at its head. On his signal, they faced each other, took hold of the coffin and lifted Carter up onto their shoulders. Then, slowly, they made their way past the platoon and up into the dark belly of the Chinook for the coffin's repatriation to the UK.

Liam stared as the rotors gathered speed and then, almost impossibly, lifted the huge beast of a craft up into the air with consummate grace. Death was something every soldier knew was a risk of the job and Liam had faced it more times than he'd dared count. From his two tours in Afghanistan to what had gone down in Kenya, it was a reality that he had been forced to deal with. But it didn't make it any easier saying farewell to another mate gone in the line of duty.

With the Chinook fading from sight, the platoon fell out and everyone quietly made their way back to anything that would take their mind off Carter's death.

Liam walked over to where he had been sleeping for the past few nights. After his ordeal, the general order had been to rest and recuperate, and that was exactly what he'd done, allowing his body to finally recover and heal. He still ached, and the cuts and grazes that covered his body were scabbing over, but he was alive, and it could so easily have turned out differently.

A voice called his name and he stopped. Odull was walking towards him, his brother at his side. They ducked into the dorm tent.

Liam smiled. 'Your mum will be pleased,' he said.

Odull laughed. 'Yes, she now has the ugly one to worry about again, not just me!'

Liam reached a hand out to Odull's brother, who took it and shook it warmly. '*He's* definitely the ugly one,' joked Liam, nodding to his friend. Then he saw Pearce making his way over on crutches, his left foot bandaged up. 'You're making a lot of fuss over just a sprain,' said Liam, as Pearce dropped down onto his own bed. 'Must be going soft.'

'It's all for show,' said Pearce. 'The ladies love a man on crutches. Appeals to their caring side.'

Odull and his brother went back to the other KDF soldiers as Liam and Pearce chatted on.

'And BATUK is just rammed with ladies,' said Liam as Cordner came in. 'Oh look, here's one now. Just your type too.'

'It's that sweet Irish lilt,' said Pearce. 'Melts a man's heart.'

'Biggs is looking for you, RB,' said Cordner.

'Really? What for?'

'Didn't tell me,' said Cordner. 'Told him you were probably over here. He was talking to Young.'

'Oh, so it's a secret,' said Pearce. 'What've you been up to now?'

Liam was about to say he hadn't a clue and wasn't much fussed, when in walked the sergeant.

'Here he is,' said Cordner. 'Just like I said. Typical of

RB, really, to be lounging about doing nothing. He's a slacker, Sergeant. Frankly, I'm sick of having to cover for him and so is Pearce.'

Sergeant Biggs walked over and sat down on his own bed.

'So what did you want to see me for?' Liam asked.

'Just a bit of news, that's all,' said Biggs. 'Just been speaking to Captain Owusu and the lieutenant.'

'You're pregnant, aren't you?' said Pearce.

'Oh, it's more serious than that,' said Biggs, and looked over to Liam with a grin creeping across his usually stony face.

'Well, whatever it is, just tell me,' said Liam.

'You've been recommended for a Gallantry Award,' said Biggs. 'It seems that the powers that be want a few more people to notice what you've been up to.'

Pearce and Cordner laughed.

'Fuck me, a medal!' said Pearce. 'You'll be able to start a collection soon!'

Liam was stunned. 'Are you serious?'

Biggs nodded. 'You deserve it, so don't go thinking otherwise. Your actions not only got us out of the shit, they brought about the apprehension of Azeez. And that's a big deal. A key player like him is a gold mine of information. Not only that, without him running the show, Al Shabaab will be a little lost, at least for a while. The KDF can use that to their advantage.'

Liam fell quiet. A few months back, he'd been questioning his decision to go for Recce Platoon; now here he was, up for a medal. If there was any confirmation needed that he was in the right job, then this was it.

'A medal,' he said. 'So I'll have to go and see the Royal Family again, I guess.'

'Yeah, tough life,' said Cordner. 'Must be terrible.'

Liam shrugged. Being recommended for such a thing was humbling, but it wouldn't bring Carter back. And as far as he was concerned, they all deserved one after what they'd been through. So why should he be singled out?

Rising from his bed, he watched as Biggs, Cordner and Pearce walked away chatting. Medals weren't easy to get, and were often given in recognition of achieving something against the odds. Liam had no problem with that – after all, the life of a soldier was a dangerous one. But more than ever, he was struck by just how quickly things could change.

What enemy would he face next?

Liam had no answers. But he realized then that he didn't really want them.

He was a soldier. And a damned good one at that.

Yes, it was an uncertain life – but he had never felt more alive.

Bring it – he was ready . . .

ANDY McNAB
DOESN'T JUST WRITE ABOUT ACTION:
HE LIVES IT

THE INCREDIBLE BESTSELLER FROM THE AUTHOR OF *BRAVO TWO ZERO*

ANDY McNAB
DCM MM
IMMEDIATE ACTION

Read this extract from Andy's
autobiography, IMMEDIATE ACTION,
and see how he responded to
a real-life hostage rescue mission

One of the scaleys (*signallers*) came in while I was still eating.

'Can we have both teams in the briefing room at 1930 for an update, I thank you!'

We sat down in front of the slime (*Int Corps personnel*) and finished off our dinner.

'We still have seen only X-ray (*terrorist*) Two. All the negotiations are still being conducted by the woman.'

We could hear her voice on the loudspeakers.

'Can you turn that up!' someone shouted from the back of the team.

The terrorist's words filled the room: 'If you do not put our statement on the BBC 9 p.m. and ITN 10 p.m. news we will start to kill people. We have shown you that we are not savages, you have your old man and children . . .'

'I want to help you,' said one of the negotiators. 'None of us want this to turn out a bloodbath, do we? I cannot make any promises, but I assure you that I am making all efforts to help you. Everything I said I would do has happened. We need to work together . . . you must understand I need time.'

'It is obvious you are not listening. We will start to kill if the broadcasts are . . .'

Somebody turned the volume down.

The slime continued: 'As you heard, the old man and two children have just been released. He is in shock and cannot give any information of any use apart from that he thinks there are four or five and only one of them a woman.'

One of the scaleys shouted out: 'Stand to the IA!'

We ran to the vehicles and turned our radios on. Weapons were made ready and respirators put on while we screamed off to the start line. The people with the entry charges were checking to ensure they were OK, and putting on the claymore clacker that would initiate the charge.

'Alpha, Tango One and Two at the start line, over.'

'Roger that, out to you. One, this is Alpha, over.'

'One, rotors turning and stood to, over.'

'Roger that, out.'

On the net, we could all hear the snipers giving information on the target: 'More movement on White Two One and White One One. There is screaming coming from the ground floor, I can't tell what room.'

'Roger that, Sierra Two.'

I heard two bursts of automatic fire and knew it

wouldn't be long before we went into action to rescue the hostages.

'Hello, One and One Alpha, this is Alpha One. Move to your holding area.'

'One, roger.'

We could not see them, but we knew that both helis would now be flying off to an area where they couldn't be heard by the terrorists, waiting for the order to move on target. It was dark by now and all lights were out. Steve and Jerry would be using their NVGs.

The chief constable now had to wait for confirmation that people had been killed. The sound of shots was not enough.

He was soon to have his confirmation: a body was dumped at the main door with the threat of another one in five minutes if the TV statement demand was not met.

The policeman spoke to COBR (*Cabinet Office Briefing Room*) and the decision was made.

The squadron OC (*officer commanding*) got on the net: 'Hello, all stations, this is Alpha One, radio check, over.'

We all answered.

'All stations, I have control, I have control. Callsigns One and One Alpha, commence your run in.'

'One and One Alpha, roger that, out.'

It was on.

The helis dropped low over the trees, still on their

NVGs. The doors both sides of the Agusta 109s were open. Each helicopter had four men aboard. The No. 1, who was going to come down the fast rope, was looking out of the helicopter as it screamed in, respirator on, looking at the approach. He had two hands on the fast rope, which was six inches in diameter. The rest of the rope dangled around his right foot ready for him to kick it out; he'd put two hands around it, grip also with the sides of his assault boots, and slide down, very much like a fireman coming down a pole.

'That's thirty seconds, thirty seconds.'

This was the last chance to cancel. The OC would have looked at the policeman for confirmation.

'All stations, I have control. Stand by, stand by . . . go, go, go!'

The vehicles moved off with the teams holding on for grim death. As we turned the corner we could see the building; Tango Two came up level with us and I heard the helis making their approach. They were flying low towards the building; lower than the building itself.

A little arm sticks out from each side of the aircraft with the fast rope; as soon as the helicopter starts to hover over the target the No. 1 kicks out the rope. As soon as the rope goes out the No. 1 goes with it; he slides down the fast rope before it hits the bottom of the roof.

I looked up. The helicopters were coming in, lots of noise, lots of downblast, shit flying off the roof. They flared just ten feet above the roof. There were flashbangs exploding, and by now the pilots have taken their NVGs off. The instruments are on a swivel on their helmets; they just push them up above their helmets as NVGs are affected by flashbangs and would be whited out.

The helicopters were straining in a flare position, then started going backwards and forwards two or three feet in a hover. The blokes were streaming down the rope. The No. 3 on each team had quite a task, because as he fast-roped, as well as his equipment, he would be bringing down a rectangular charge over his shoulder. He'd have to be really careful with it so he didn't rip off the det or mess up the wiring.

At one time there were all four of them on the fast rope. As soon as each man's feet hit the bottom he moved out of the way. As they came down they were looking around, looking at the floor, making sure nobody was coming out of the skylights to start taking a pop at them.

Seconds later, the helis were gone.

Someone put his head out of the top left-hand window; we knew Sierra One had him in his sights; there was no need for us to worry, that was his job. He didn't get on the radio, he just got his telescopic sight on him, covering the assault as it went in. If he was a threat he would soon have a 7.62 Lapua round in his head to make sure he stopped being one.

On the Standby the other two snipers around the back, Sierra Three and Four, had gone running forward with G3s, choosing areas where they could cover two sides each. They didn't need telescopic sights because they were so close; their G3s had normal iron sights. They had the outside covered, they could take any runners that were coming out. If the X-rays ran out beyond the snipers they'd get caught in the police cordon, but that never came into the equation; as somebody in B Squadron once said, no one runs faster than Mr Heckler & Koch.

As the Range Rover stopped, flashbangs were going off.

We jumped off and ran to the main doors. They were locked and still covered over with curtains. Dave secured the charge to the left-hand side door with double-sided tape; there was enough explosive to blow the whole thing in.

Everyone was back against the wall, looking up with weapons covering the windows. If anyone poked their head out with bad intentions they would not enjoy the view for long.

As he moved back, Dave checked with his hand the line of the det cord to the detonator, and then to the firing wire, a last check to make sure everything was right. By checking, he could say, 'Bin it,' if it was screwed up and we'd go straight in with the axes, just as Tiny had had to do at the Embassy. He was rushing, but he was still taking his time to make sure the charge was complete. The last thing he wanted to do was push that clacker and have nothing happen.

Both teams were ready. As Dave went past, Tim, the No. 2, was ready with another flashbang.

I had my weapon up in the aim, ready to go in. As I took off the safety, I shouted, 'Go!'

Our charge and one of the first-floor team's went off at the same time. I started to move. The flashbang flew past me and I followed it in: it would be no good going in after it had finished, I had to be there with it.

The hallway was dark and was starting to fill with smoke from the flashbangs. Another one exploded and I felt the effect of the blast. The noise jarred my whole body and I could feel the pressure on my eardrums. The flash was blinding but I had to work through that. We'd trained enough in these situations; my hands still carried burn marks from when one of the maroons had hit me.

The whole building was shaking with concussion and seared by sheets of blinding light.

On my right I could see the other team moving. I didn't look but I knew that my group would be heading for that first door.

The hallway was clear.

I turned and saw that I was No. 2 at the door. The last two of my lot had gone straight for it and were waiting. I heard flashbangs and firing from the other floors.

I ran over, pulling out a flashbang and getting right behind the first man. I put it over his shoulder so he knew that we were ready.

The No. 3 on the opposite side of us kicked the door open. As soon as four inches of gap appeared the flashbang was in and so were we.

Nobody was worried about what was inside or what would happen when the door was opened. We'd done it so many times. There was no time to think about danger or the possibility of cocking up.

The lights were on and the noise and flashes were doing their job well. Dave went left; as I came in I saw a group of people huddled together in a corner but no people with masks or weapons.

I heard an MP5 fire. One of the group pulled an AK and was bringing it up.

I got my torch onto his head and gave him a quick burst.

The Yankees (*hostages*) were screaming and crying and had to be controlled.

Tim, who was covering both of us as we took the room, shouted, 'Get down, get down!' He pointed his weapon at them to make them understand that he was serious –

and because there could be terrorists in the group.

He was now dragging them down onto the floor if they weren't doing what they were told. This was no time to be sensitive and caring.

Dave moved forward at the same time to clear the room. Because he had to move a settee he let his weapon go on its sling and pulled his pistol.

At the same time Tim was shouting: 'Where are the terrorists, any more terrorists?'

Once we cleared the room we were going to the next one. As I came out Tim was pushing people onto the floor and shouting, 'Stay there, don't move!'

The other teams were still doing their stuff. I ran past our No. 4, who was covering the hallway. He was in a corner so that he dominated the whole area and at the same time could see up the staircase.

I got to the door and became No. 1. The bottom of my respirator had filled up with sweat and I was breathing so heavily under all the body armour that I could feel its diaphragm clanking up and down. Tim came up behind me and shoved a flashbang under my nose. Once we had a No. 3 we were ready and in we went.

The room was empty.

Shouts echoed from other rooms as the Yankees were controlled. My breathing was laboured, I was listening to the net, listening to two lots of people speaking at once.

Oral commands were being shouted through respirators; hand signals were flashing from man to man. Throughout the building there were weapons firing, maroons exploding, smoke and people everywhere.

It was very claustrophobic inside the respirator. I was a big sweaty mess, trying to do my job and think of about ten things at the same time.

We still had a problem. We didn't know if any X-rays had hidden among the Yankees – or maybe the Yankees were actively shielding some. The Stockholm Syndrome bonds victims to their captors; they had to be covered with weapons until we knew who was who.

Tim started to move up the stairs, covered by a member from the other team. He moved very slowly, his pistol out, ready. He was making sure there was no threat on the stairs, and ensuring that he didn't have a blue-on-blue with the other link man he was to RV with. They linked up and I got on the net.

It had been just over two minutes from the 'Go, go, go!' The firing had stopped but the shouting had not. Smoke was billowing everywhere and now all the callsigns were sending information back on the net that their areas were clear and what the casualty state was.

Fat Boy said, 'We have a wounded woman.'

I looked around and one of the Yankees was holding her leg.

I got onto the net: 'This is Three, we have a wounded Yankee, request medic back-up, over.'

'Roger that, Three. He is on his way, out.'

Dave went to the door to lead him to the casualty. I then got on the net and gave my sitrep.

By now the whole of the front of the building was floodlit and the hostage reception were ready for custom.

'All stations, evacuate the Yankees, evacuate the Yankees.'

It looked like a human conveyor belt as we moved people out. They mustn't have time to think, they must be scared; you shout and holler to control them into the arms of the hostage reception. Everybody was picking them up and shoving them, shouting: 'Get up, get up! Move, move, move!'

They got as hard a time as if they were confirmed terrorists, lined up face down on the floor and hand-cuffed.

'Stay still, no talking!'

They were covered with pistols.

The SSM came along with a torch, grasped hold of each person's head and pulled it back, shining the powerful beam into their eyes. 'Name?'

When he was satisfied that everyone was who they said they were, they were put on transport and moved away to the police cordon.

'Hello, Alpha One, this is Two. We have a possible IED. We have marked it and are moving out. Over.'

They would put a small flashing yellow light on it. The same would be done for a man down; yellow light penetrates smoke better than white.

Someone else was getting direction from CRW.

'Alpha One, roger. RV with ATO, all callsigns evacuate the building, over.'

We all acknowledged, quite pleased to be evacuating. We could get back to the admin area, have a quick debrief, and then it would be wacky races back to Hereford. There was a great rule that whoever came on the helis went back on them. That was fine, apart from having to listen to Steve bang on about his latest squash game.

The exercise had gone smoothly. We'd been good, and so we should have been. We were on the ranges every day, leaping onto buildings, screaming through the CQB house, running around with the vehicles, up and down ladders, practising until we could almost do it blindfolded. The only thing that didn't improve with the training was that we lived our lives with a ring around our faces where the seal of the respirator pressed down.